D0196932

THE TROLLEY

ALSO BY CLAUDE SIMON, TRANSLATED BY
RICHARD HOWARD

The Wind

The Grass

The Flanders Road

The Palace

History

The Battle of Pharsalus

The Acacia

THE TROLLEY

CLAUDE SIMON

Translated from the French by Richard Howard

THE NEW PRESS • NEW YORK

Originally published as *Le Tramway* by Les Éditions de Minuit, 2001
Published in the United States by The New Press, New York, 2002
Distributed by W. W. Norton & Company, Inc., New York

LIBRARY OF CONGRESS CATALOGING-IN-PUBLICATION DATA

Simon, Claude.
    [Tramway. English]
    The trolley / Claude Simon;
  translated from the French by Richard Howard.
        p. cm.
     ISBN 1-56584-734-2 (hc)
       1. Howard, Richard, 1929- II. Title.

PQ2637.I547 T6813 2002
843'.914—dc21

                                           2002019026

The New Press was established in 1990 as a not-for-profit alternative to
the large, commercial publishing houses currently dominating the
book publishing industry. The New Press operates in the public interest
rather than for private gain, and is committed to publishing, in
innovative ways, works of educational, cultural, and
community value that are often deemed insufficiently profitable.

The New Press, 450 West 41st Street, 6th floor, New York, NY 10036
www.thenewpress.com

Printed in the United States of America

2   4   6   8   10   9   7   5   3   1

To Réa, again

... for him the meaning of an episode is not to be found within it, as inside a nut, but outside, enveloping the tale which has generated it as a light generates a vapor ... JOSEPH CONRAD

... since an image is the essential element, a simplification entirely suppressing real characters would be a decisive improvement. MARCEL PROUST

THE TROLLEY

$\mathcal{T}$HE NEEDLE POINTING TO AN ARC OF EMBOSSED bronze gradations on the dial responded to a lever the motorman tapped with his open palm in order to start moving or gain speed, returning it to its initial position and thus cutting the current when approaching a stop, then rapidly and strenuously turning a cast-iron wheel to his right (a smaller version of the kind which used to work well-pumps in old-time kitchens) in order to activate the screeching brakes. The handle of the lever which the motorman pushed as he stood in front of the oval column on which this rudimentary instrument-panel was set retained only a faint brown trace of its original varnish, the unprotected wood beneath now grayish and probably grimy.

To ride in the motorman's cab (which in any case you had to step through in order to enter the tram proper) instead of taking a seat on the benches inside constituted something of a privilege not only to my child's mind but also, quite plainly, to those of the two or three passengers who, similarly scorning the benches, would stand as a rule in the cab, probably not imbued like me with the importance of their position but simply because smoking was permitted here, judging by the apparently taciturn motorman who may have been "officially" silent as enjoined by a sort of Franco-English placard: "Défense de Parler au Wattman," which somehow reduced him to an inferior caste, condemned to mute solitude, at the same time that it suffused him with a nimbus of power like those tragedy kings or potentates it was forbidden by a severe (and sometimes mortal) protocol to address directly, a status (or position—or function) the motorman assumed with utmost gravity, eyes always fixed on the oncoming rails, as if absorbed by the weight of his responsibility, waiting at each stop for the liberating clang of the ticket-taker's bell to re-ignite, with his nickel-plated lighter, the cigarette butt stuck to his lower lip for the entire route (which from beach to town required, including stops, about three-quarters of an hour), a stubby grayish tube of saliva-steeped paper which had turned transparent around the brown tobacco it contained and was nearly split by the rough stems (known as "logs") which were too thick or unevenly rolled.

I seemed to see it, to be there among the two or three privileged characters permitted to stand in the cramped six-foot-square cab provided they neither addressed nor distracted the silent motorman in a gray flannel shirt buttoned to the neck, threadbare trousers, and rope-soled espadrilles not exactly down at the heels but so frayed they seemed bearded, standing with feet wide apart and the impassive face and extinguished cigarette of a quasi-

mythic being whose gestures—at least to my child's eyes—
seemed to have something ritualistic and sacred about
them as he tapped the speed-lever with his open palm,
leaned over to yank the brake-wheel, or stamped his right
foot on the warning-whistle button as the car took a blind
curve, sounding it almost continuously when, once past
the tollhouse, the tram entered the town proper, first de-
scending the long slope to the public gardens, skirting the
wall around them, turning left at the monument to the
war dead and, following the Boulevard du Président Wilson, gradually slowed along the Allée des Marronniers,
coming to a stop at the end of the line almost in the center
of town, opposite the movie-house with its glass marquee
and enticing posters which in garish colors offered pro-
spective customers the enormous faces of women with
disheveled hair, heads flung back and mouths open wide
in a scream of terror or the invitation to a kiss.

Some fifteen kilometers separated the beach from town:
a rolling landscape with vine-covered slopes, the route
dotted (on the right side as you came up from the beach)
with opulent estates, their houses dating from the last
century, two or three kilometers apart and somewhat
concealed by trees, offering an inventory of what the van-
ity of recently acquired or consolidated fortunes could
inspire in their owners, as well as in the architects who
complied with (or even anticipated) their wishes to build
at a period when the ambitions of a wealthy provincial
class of limited cultural resources (occasionally inspired

by the medieval or orientalist décors of operas seen in Paris during a honeymoon, for example) proposed a range of architectural features (towers crowned with delicate terra-cotta balustrades or else squat, flat-topped, and vaguely Saracen), of questionable taste but generally agreeable, not too embarrassingly ostentatious (except for one, the most recent), with old-fashioned names (like their Louis-Philippe or Napoléon III furniture) and a certain naive freshness (like "Miraflores" or, more simply, "The Aloes").

In either direction (from town to shore or the reverse) two trolleys leaving once an hour at the same time passed each other halfway along the route, not far in fact from that property the name of which ("Joué") matched an absurd crenellated façade (like those cardboard toys, those forts or castles given to children as Christmas presents), and vague misgivings still clung to the origins and date of the builder's fortune, the present inhabitants (descendants of the romantic parvenu or perhaps recent purchasers) treated by the little society of the other "estates" not with any sort of ostracism but quite simply ignored, which somehow afforded them a certain prestige consisting of a combination of scorn and suspicion, the latter encouraged by the fact that from a certain angle, before the trolley took the incline leading to the "garage" (the name given to the double set of tracks which, halfway up the line, permitted the two cars to pass each other), it was evident that the ridiculous medieval façade was attached to nothing but an unfinished, not even roughcast wall behind which could be momentarily glimpsed a huge windowless structure (really a sort of shed), so that the tile roof had to slope down to accommodate what passed for medieval loopholes in the crenellated architecture.

At this hour of the morning, the two or three schoolboys allowed to stand in the narrow and prestigious cab were trying to avoid notice by standing close together in order to make room for those other habitués, apparently office workers or laborers in threadbare clothes just like the motorman's and who preferred to ride standing in the cab, exchanging an occasional remark in this congested place where they were permitted to smoke or rather to suck on the cigarette butts rolled in that same grayish paper made transparent by saliva: a taciturn group to which, years later, I would recall belonging with that same sense of absurd privilege (though realizing I was being shown no more than tolerance), a sort of elite in the stifling stench of the shed vestibule which the guards locked up at night and in which every afternoon there would be five or six shadowy figures in clothes just as threadbare and dirty as the motorman's (with this difference, that they (the clothes) had once been uniforms and that, in the stench of the field latrines which were also set up in that airless vestibule where their presence was tolerated, their elitism consisted solely in the possession by cunning, theft or some clandestine trafficking, of the sole mercantile value acknowledged in such a place, i.e. (as was indicated by similar hand-rolled cigarette butts, lumpy, spit-drenched and smoked down to the very end), of tobacco). And in the same way, having reached the end of the line, the motorman, head tilted to avoid the flame of the lighter so close to his lips, drew one last puff on that cigarette butt reduced to less than a centimeter of black-rimmed paper which glowed for a second before being delicately grasped between two fingers, plucked from his lower lip to which it had stuck, and finally thrown away, after which, holding in one hand the lever-handle raised off its axis, he stepped down from the car and, accompanied by the ticket-taker, headed for the little cement pavilion evidently built on the model of the comfort stations (a function it would in part subserve) and which doubtless included a narrow desk covered with log books to be signed and a cash box for the ticket-taker, both men covering the several yards like a sort of twin figure, with this difference that if the ticket-taker seemed to be wearing the same shapeless gray outfit he was nonetheless distinguished from the motorman by a sort of military cap, and his shapeless jacket was creased by the shoulder strap of his coin purse as well as by the strap of his oblong ticket tray held in the crook of his left elbow and on which were stacked in two parallel rows the many-colored stubs of the (one-way / round-trip) tickets corresponding to each of the stops along the route in a range of pastel colors (pink, tan, mauve, yellow, orange, indigo, azure) which, contrasting with the taciturn and expressionless faces of the two men and their threadbare garments, seemed like a bright display of flowers, their price-stamped petals sanguine and primaveral in every season.

That Allée des Marronniers which the trolley followed, gradually slowing down at the end of its route, parallel to the Boulevard du Président Wilson just past the monument to the dead erected at the entrance to the municipal gardens, seemed to constitute, in the late afternoons (as if there were a link between them and the monumental monument), the rendezvous of half a dozen of those little go-carts consisting of a black-painted wicker seat between two wheels behind a third smaller wheel attached to a steering-shaft by a bicycle-chain running up to the double-crank also serving as handlebars and operated by the hands of those men (or rather, apparently, of exact copies of the same man—for they all looked just alike: the same bony, raptorial countenance, the same black moustache waxed to a point (or comically frizzled with a hot curling-iron), the same hand-rolled cigarette butt, the same tiny fan of faded ribbons in the jacket buttonhole, the same shiny black oilcloth, creased and worn in patches, spreading from the seat down to the narrow running-board on which no foot ever rested) whom Maman called with what seemed a sort of wicked delight by a compound name (*stump-men*) which had a sort of sinister resonance (like *thousand-legger* or *praying-mantis*) and which on her lips and in her tone of voice had something at once offensive, macabre, and despairing about it, as if she were reproaching them not only for the exhibition of their infirmity, but for merely existing, for having emerged, virtually sliced in two but alive, from that conflict which had torn from her the only man she had ever loved, as if that cruel label of hers somehow implied a charge of cowardice along with envy, jealousy, and pity—she who had now renounced that crepe veil behind which, not without a certain ostentation, she had hidden her face long past the decent limits of mourning, but persisted in wearing only dark colors and who perhaps (just as her membership in a certain charitable society obliged her twice a week to teach the catechism to a handful of unruly children in a side-chapel of the cathedral) visited the hospital or the hospice or the asylum (there must have been a site, a shared locus from which, in the late afternoons, they headed toward that Allée des Marronniers impassive and terrifying with their waxed moustaches, their hawklike noses, their rickety vehicles and their tormented bodies, constituting a permanent chastisement, a permanent recrimination with regard to the living . . .) where these wretched creatures were quartered, in order to bring them candy or even perhaps (though she hated this vice, but doubtless in memory of that smoking-service brought back from the Orient by the man for whom she still wore mourning and which figured in cloisonné (tray, tobacco jar and ashtrays) a flock of pink-breasted turquoise birds flying through reeds over huge water-lilies) . . . perhaps, then, some of that inferior tobacco stocked in country stores, cubical packets wrapped

in flimsy gray paper sealed by the white ribbon of the State
Excise, and to which she never failed to attach one of those
notebooks of little sheets of cigarette paper whose trade-
marks ("Riz-la-Croix" or "JOB") might have seemed so
many incitations to submit to their martyrdom had not
the cross stamped on sky-blue paper simply referred to a
manufacturer's name and the acronym JOB printed in
gold letters on a white background been derived, as was
common knowledge, from the lozenge-shaped enlarge-
ment of the founder of the firm's initials (one Joseph Bar-
dou) and, like the cross, had no application to the
sufferings of the biblical figure.

Furthermore, her own face (which when she was still a
young woman had begun to grow puffy during the four
years of an interminable engagement when she had ob-
stinately opposed her mother in order to insist upon mar-
riage with a penniless man, a match which the old lady
considered if not degrading at the very least disastrous
socially as well as financially, and which, later on, disappointment or rather despair, the accumulation of tears,
seemed to have distended even more, filling it like a
sponge) . . . her own face, then, since the disease which
was to carry him off had attacked her, proceeded, as
though by a sort of mimetism (or macabre coquetry) at
first simply to waste away, then to grow cadaverous and
gradually to mummify, irresistibly suggesting by the end,
in an ashen, feminized, and pitiless form, the faces of
those men physically amputated of half of themselves and,

as if she was blaming them for some indecent exhibitionism or even, who knows? despite their cruel mutilation (one of them had only one arm as well) for still being alive—or rather for having survived, for having emerged from that war which had torn half of herself from her as well, so that this horrifying label of *stump-men* which turned them into somehow mythical creatures (half-human, half-arboreal) and which she never failed to repeat on each occasion with a certain insistence and even satisfaction ("the stump-men's allée," "that time of the afternoon when the stump-men get together," etc.), seemed like an unappeasable protest, as if she had perceived their existence (or their perseverance in remaining alive) as an affront to her grief, a ceaselessly renewed sneer of fate, and . . .

And again it happened, not abruptly but somehow insidiously, so that when I became aware of it the thing had already begun, gradually squeezing my arm like a sort of reptile coiled around itself in overlapping rings, perhaps for the second or third time since I had been there, realizing now that its onset must obey some automatic recording mechanism like those barometric curves registered on the slowly revolving cylinder displayed in certain cabinets of precision instruments, wondering vaguely (but I was not in pain) if someone in the hospital was responsible for supervising these mechanisms every hour or so, ready to intervene, or if they merely glanced at them just before morning rounds: but I was not in pain, lying on my back, the sheet pulled up to my chin, unable to sleep since I can only fall asleep on my side, realizing then that I had not slept but had simply forgotten or maybe it was the fever for now they had closed the door (or rather the double doors through which a wheeled bed could pass) where through a sort of oval porthole in the upper half I could nonetheless see despite the dim light the four letters RANS above the door of the room opposite, remembering then the whole word (TRANSIT) which I had managed to read a little earlier when the doors of both rooms were still open, even remembering that opposite me was TRANSIT 1 and that consequently I must be in TRANSIT 2, but just for the night, a temporary assignment as the intern had explained to me, sent to Emergency on account of my late arrival until tomorrow when I could be transferred to the service (another building?) where I would be treated, and doubtless the same was true of the occupant of TRANSIT 1 whom for all the time the double doors had stayed open I could see lying just opposite me: a woman judging by the quantity of blond hair spread over the pillow around a face (or rather around a mask, so motionless it seemed, so lifeless), strangely pink (or turned pink by the light), its features, from where I was lying, indistinguishable, but particularly striking by its complete immobility for all the time I could see it (i.e., the time the respective doors of the two TRANSIT rooms were left open) and also because a square pillow of which the face occupied the exact center was arranged with one corner at the top like an ace of diamonds, wondering whether the patient had requested this odd arrangement or if the medical demands of the case (though how could this be?) required such a thing, and all the more intrigued by that loose hair, that pink absolutely inexpressive mask, and that arrangement of the pillow since it seemed to me, while I passed on my wheeled bed through the sort of vestibule off which the two TRANSIT rooms opened (but was this another effect of the fever?) I had glimpsed the figures of two uniformed policemen sitting in a shadowy corner, wondering (trying to shift those things behind my ears which were hurting me, my fingers groping, finding the slender tubes, following them to my nostrils, thinking Ah oxygen, good!) ... wondering again what the two policemen could be doing there (observing the sick woman with an overly pink expressionless face or protecting her? ...), thinking But maybe I didn't see things right I'm getting mixed up thinking That fucking fever, thinking ... Then too exhausted to sustain the effort of thinking, resigning myself to that sort of mire, of mist with no before no after (one, two hours earlier? ...) when the figures of two policemen gesticulating, supporting more than leading not the usual ragged and red-faced bum with a three-day beard, staggering more than struggling, protesting hoarsely, but a man still young and prop-

erly dressed though without an overcoat on this cool
March night when the air was quite sharp, while the three
figures came pitching down between the two rows of
"emergency" beds lined up along the corridor walls, like
the sudden noisy intrusion of the world of the living into
its contrary, followed in silence by twenty pairs of expressionless eyes in equally expressionless faces, not so
much empty as absent, which the clownish quality of the
scene did not alter by a single smile, not even by a mo-
mentary twitching of the lips . . .

Yet (in contrast to the habitués in their threadbare uniforms shut up in the airless vestibule stinking of ammonia
and despite the fact that like the motorman the two or
three riders standing in the cab were occasionally puffing
on similar cigarette butts) it was not (since they themselves were not smoking) the possession of tobacco which
conferred on the schoolboys also allowed to ride there
that feeling of belonging to a sort of club of initiates but
rather, beyond the fact of finding themselves so to speak
at the very heart of the control station, the phenomenon
of being in close contact (at this hour of the morning
when the trolley clientele for the most part consisted of
manual laborers and servants sent to town to do the shop-
ping) with people altogether different from those (parents, friends) they were used to seeing around them, so

that, in addition to the fact that these elect would now and then exchange with the motorman, despite the explicit prohibition to do so, some unintelligible and seemingly confidential remarks, they (the schoolboys) felt themselves somehow to be members of a secret and exclusive confraternity which had admitted them into its intimacy.

... And not even when a moment later, being violently pushed open, the door of the room (reception? first aid?) into which the trio had vanished, closing on a confused hubbub of voices exploding anew when the drunkard, doubled over, burst in again, one of his temples split like a ripe fruit now swabbed with mercurochrome, pursued by the policeman and the intern whose white coat floated behind him, already galloping (the drunkard) while clumsily trying to stuff his unbuttoned shirt into his trousers, his voice (distinct now, high, outraged) saying That that's not right, you've got ... having no time to finish, caught up with by his pursuers who were openly laughing now and making conciliatory remarks, grabbing him, pushing him back into the little room its door pulled shut by the last man under the still-inexpressive, identical stares of the motionless somehow absent masks waiting there as though stricken with a sort of paralysis, as if what united them at that moment was not so much their almost forgotten physical suffering, relegated to the background by suffering of another order, as if they had acceded to another state of being following the shared experience each of them had just lived through, which was to be abruptly snatched or rather extirpated from the familiar, reassuring and complex world in which they had heretofore existed and conveyed at tremendous speed, lying with their arms at their sides and their feet toward the rear doors of an ambulance (a sort of coffin) through the windows of which they could see vanishing vertiginously into the gray evening the confused succession of façades, crossroads, red lights, shop windows and brightly lighted cafés, everything somehow suddenly appearing, surging up out of that mystery toward which they were being swept, swaying, escaping and vanishing into a sort of tunnel, a black and bottomless perspective.

... Trolley which often, breathless from running, I despaired to see, already at the end of the Boulevard du Président Wilson, turning right and disappearing, despite the repeated protests of the parents of several schoolboys who, like myself, finished class at four o'clock, and who had requested the Company to delay the scheduled departure another five minutes, a request the Company seemed to have granted (or had merely pretended to?)— unless that departure on the stroke of four, which was generally what happened, was the result of a certain deliberate hostility on the part of the employees thereby offering a sort of double defiance: on the one hand to the Company itself which may have penalized them as well at some time in the past for being late, and on the other hand to the owners of those opulent estates whose children were receiving the advantages of an education their own modest origins had denied them. In any case it turned out that the two or three breathless schoolboys (all of them excused, by their parents' request to the principal, some five minutes before the end of class but mischievously detained until it was too late by some instructor (specifically the history and geography prof) who similarly nursed toward the affluent citizens (for reasons perhaps not so different, the clothes one of them was wearing being almost as threadbare as those of the trolley employees—but formulated (or justified) in a language quite obviously unknown to the latter) a resentment equivalent to that of the "wattmen") ... breathless, the schoolboys reluctantly (for "causing disorder") excused (relegated, with a view to this anticipated departure, to the last rows of seats in the classroom reserved for dunces) five minutes before the end of class, which, added to the minutes requested by their parents, would have amounted to ten, more than sufficient time for them to gather their notebooks, to leave (discreetly and without making too much noise, as the history and geography prof stipulated) their classrooms, to dash across the school grounds, past the

courthouse, across the square where the statue stood, to
follow, still running, the Quai de la Préfecture in order to
emerge at last in front of the rococo façade of the movie-
house and see the trolley vanishing in the distance, the
schoolboys standing there, panting, not so much disap-
pointed as humiliated, as if (according to the habit of
attributing to things or to mechanisms the thoughts or
intentions proper to human beings) . . . as if the trolley
itself were disappearing with a sort of mocking and ma-
licious sneer, leaving them standing there holding their
heavy school satchels, with the prospect of an hour not
to be killed before the next trolley left but to be filled, i.e.
by loitering in front of the closed doors of the movie-
house (where behind panes of glass the pale green notice
which announced in alluring terms but in tiny letters the
action of the week's film was surrounded by black-and-
white photographs presumed to be equally alluring of the
chief scenes in which the actors in frozen attitudes
stripped of the magic of movement on the silvery shim-
mer of the screen corresponded in only the most disap-
pointing manner to the promises of the huge posters
where the giant and impassioned faces appeared in a riot
of garish colors), or (but they had only a little change in
their pockets) among the harsh stale smells of acetylene
and caramels putrefying among the fairground stalls set
up every autumn under the plane trees along the Allée
des Marronniers where, in the melancholy twilight, the
tempting lights of the carousels and other attractions

flickered, chief among which (after the forbidden mysteries of the Musée Dupuytren) were those Russian Mountains which, dispersing for a whole month the little gathering of stump-men, raised their intricate scaffoldings from which the disastrous roar of the plummeting cars and the shrill screams of the women ricocheted against the high pediment of the monument to the dead.

The door above which was written TRANSIT 1 was wide open and there was no longer anyone in the newly made bed on which it seemed the night before had been lying or rather was laid not the body but the enigmatic and detached pink head, blond hair spreading on both sides of the pillow beneath it like the ace of diamonds now back in normal position. The intern who came to push my bed told me that unfortunately no private room was available but that in the one I had been assigned my sole companion would be a very old and quite peaceful old man.

Monument constructed on a pediment of the local pink sandstone and high as a two-story house, erected at the entrance to the municipal gardens and on which, against a black marble background (like a necrology announcement framed in some precious substance) extended endless columns of the names in gold leaf of the city's dead oddly symbolized in the form of three life-size figures roughly chiseled in white stone, which by means of the props they were provided with could be recognized as a fisherman with his net over one shoulder, a vine-grower with one foot on his shovel, and a mason holding a trowel, the three figures merely roughed in (deliberately? symbolically?), quite jagged (the mud of the trenches?) and which the sculptor (a member of the wealthy family which manufactured a famous apéritif) had arranged not in a row but in a shallow arc as if, unconcerned with the pedestrians or spectators, they were there not to be seen by the public but as though somehow emerging from the realm of the dead and conversing among themselves. This was the spot where, turning right and for a moment offering its flank to the view of the nonplussed schoolboys, the trolley vanished for good in that L-shaped extension of the Boulevard du Président Wilson which changing its name at this point now bore the name of only a local dignitary.

But I could not enjoy the escapes and dreams which, despite the disappointment of the photographs posted at the entrance to the movie-house, were promised by the garish posters (or the various pleasures proposed by the fairground attractions) except at a run, being obliged if I missed that four o'clock trolley to go to the house of my oldest cousin's husband already discharged from the army and set up in some sort of business in town and appointed by Maman not only to protect me from such dangers but even to see to it that I did not waste my time so that if I had to wait for the next trolley I could immediately get started on my homework or begin studying the next day's lessons. As a matter of fact he was a good-natured man, stricken with a sort of amiable melancholy, who seemed to have no other pleasure (or other means of escape) in life than to sit down at the piano beneath which he stretched out his painfully damaged left leg with its fractured kneecap, a legacy of the war, and which he played quite unpretentiously, priding himself only on giving lavish dinners when touring virtuosos passed through town. Out of kindness or weakness or timidity, he doubtless considered he had kept his promise to Maman when I was served, by one of his employees, a big cup of hot chocolate accompanied by cookies for which, as soon as I had wiped my lips with the napkin, I would thank him without even pretending to have done my homework and immediately rush down the stairs.

When I was lucky enough not to miss the four o'clock trolley (i.e. when my teacher's mood coincided with the motorman's) and I would get home rather early, the already low October sun lengthening rather ominously the shadows of the pines over the gravel path of the garden where every afternoon had been set out that chaise longue, or rather that deck chair on which lay not Maman but that sort of hawk-headed mummy whose skin was now a waxy yellow, her once Bourbon nose transformed into some kind of beak, and her gaze sharpened by pain until there was something almost irascible about it: I don't know which physician—she had been operated on in Paris by what was called at the time a pundit of surgery—had prescribed (perhaps merely to give her the illusion of a possible cure which he knew was out of the question) that she eat a certain daily amount of not rare but raw meat which she consumed in the form of tiny pellets to which she had so great a repugnance (she who had once been so greedy that she saved every menu of the elaborate dinners given by the Governor-General of the Colony and, out there, kept herself informed by the best caterer of the latest arrival of fresh lobsters) that in order to overcome it she had to do herself such violence that she seemed a macabre caricature of voracity, thrusting (as if paradoxically famished) her head forward in a fierce movement which, with that shriveled bony nose of hers, bore a certain resemblance to the two captive eagles in the municipal gardens tearing at some rotten carcass in their cage; all that was left of her maternal love being gradually transformed (as she saw inexorably approaching the moment of her death which would leave behind an orphan of eleven) into a sort of despairing violence which impelled her, doubtless in order to forestall (or to palliate) the future dangers (idleness or lack of proper training) which she presumed she had to watch out for on my behalf, to redouble her severity, as if (by an amalgamation of that piety which, I was told later on, she had somewhat

neglected during those three years of lobster-sustained or-
giastic happiness she had shared with my father on that
tropical island to which he had taken her and a doubtless
somewhat mythic notion of a certain military rigor and
an inflexible conception of honor) she had turned herself
into a figure of austere rigidity who daily made me dread
the moment of discovering her, half reclining on that deck
chair covered with toile de Jouy on which tiny baskets of
flowers arranged in quincunxes appeared between delicate
pink stripes, wearing that gray flannel bathrobe bordered
with a dark-gray braid, her shoulders always swathed in
a pale mauve shawl, and greeting me each time with that
fierce and fearful maternal adoration which led her to
overdramatize any low mark or penalty recorded on the
report card I would have to bring her.

If what might be called the domestic terminus of the
trolley line was located almost in the heart of town, at its
other end the rusty tracks disappeared, some yards after
a buffer-stop, under a layer of sand which the sea breeze
spread over them with the same patient stubbornness as
the Company laborer's whose job it was to sweep the parallel set of tracks permitting the trolley to be attached to
a trailer, called *la baladeuse*, which in summer it towed
behind it, the parallel benches of this addition enclosed
only by wooden posts which connected the floor to the
roof and between which fluttered curtains of clumsily
hung coarse cloth. A tarred wooden lean-to sheltered the
trolley at night, at the edge of the beach where the tracks

were prolonged by two narrow paths of faded grayish planks corroded by salt, they too half-buried in sand where they crossed the beach, leading to a group of similarly tarred sheds forming three sides of a quadrilateral about twenty yards wide, open to the sea and consisting of bathing huts, a bar, and a café-restaurant around a dance floor. Information gathered at secondhand, for we (children) were still forbidden to approach (a prohibition never actually specified but which was understood, following quite naturally from the way, in the family, this place was referred to, as people might speak of the disagreeable nuisance created by some factory in the neighborhood or by some malodorous garbage dump) and solely as a point of reference, for instance, to indicate the villa of certain friends—or where their habitual place on the beach was situated (either to the right or left, and always of course at some distance)—or even in speaking of some servant, some little upstairs maid or the tenant farmer's daughter who on her day off went dancing there: a place (the apparently rundown group of these brown-tarred sheds) which by a sort of ironic paradox was called "Society Beach" and which (replaced later on, but not so close to the sea and almost next to the trolley terminus, by a yellow-painted cube of concrete baptized "Casino"), though rather grim-looking, doubtless took its name not from the frequentation of "society" patrons in the decorative sense of the word, but from the fact that on holidays it attracted a lot of people, as could be judged even from a distance by the abundance or rather the swarm of tiny silhouettes or rather of tiny agglutinated dots that blackened the beach between this establishment and the shoreline—actually overflowing into the sea which seemed, as at the passage of certain schools of fish breaking the surface, to seethe, to flash here and there with little spurts of foam, but not very far from the beach, for few knew how to swim and it was even remarked with hypocritical sympathy and as a thing bordering on the comical (somewhat the way puppies might be alluded to) that every Sunday one or two people actually drowned, stricken with cramps from having gone into the water too soon after a copious repast very copiously basted with wine, the spectacle contemplated from a distance producing that rather mysterious or even rather peculiar reaction always afforded by the contrast between an intense human activity and the utter silence in which it is occurring for at a distance the wind, always perpendicular to the coast, whether coming from the east or the west, carried away all the noises, shouts, songs, music, so that to the bad reputation of the place, the lilliputian agitation seen to spangle the sea with spurts of foam, was added that quasi-disturbing element which was the total absence of sound, the tricolor always spread flat out by one of the prevailing winds and floating over that long tar-colored shed, the flag itself seeming, with the ragged fringe of its red stripe, the unreal and clandestine standard of an activity or of pleasures themselves unreal and clandestine, as if the trolley line had been built by the Company only to link these two poles of popular attraction consisting on the one hand of the movie-house with its garish posters and on the other this "society beach" ministering in passing to these arrogant country houses concealing their crenellations and their towers (and in some cases their decrepitude—if not their dilapidation) behind their screens of pines, summer residences of more or less (and sometimes not at all) prosperous families but who (custom or pride) from July to September erected here and there on the wide beach tiny structures called "shelters" but which, consisting of a solid carcass of rafters and planks over which were stretched striped tarpaulins, once bright-colored but gradually faded by the salt, being in fact (the side facing the sea being always open) so many little living rooms where the mothers of the neighborhood visited one another and had their salons, as they called it, while knitting or sewing something and keeping an eye on the children bathing: "It's always so nice at the shore Madame Espinosa came to visit Maman yesterday but Gaguy has a sore throat when are you going back?" the calling card on the back of which these words were scribbled in chaotic and swooping lines representing, behind a little undulation of dunes, a series of one-story bungalows with hideous roofs of mass-produced tiles aspiring no doubt to the pretentious appellation of "villas" as was attested to by the unexpected architectural embellishments (such as a medieval watchtower on the corner of one of these ...) As for that Madame Espinosa (owner of one of these pavilions where one year, for the month of August, in order to be close to her sister who had installed her numerous family in the only one of these villas that could contain them all (a huge one-story barrack, this one in Norman style, all slate and half-timbering), Maman had rented two rooms from her, their floor tiles slippery with sand and affording the most rudimentary comfort—I can still see moving with extraordinary speed across the bedroom wall, as we were getting ready for bed, a huge pale-yellow thousand-legger surrounded by an undulating fringe of agile limbs, which after a long pursuit one of my cousins who had run after it finally managed to cut in half) ... as for that Madame Espinosa, the mother of little Gaguy, our playmate whose indisposition my young cousin had already told me about, this was a sort of beach acquaintance who, if she was received in her salon-shelter by my aunt, was never invited to the musical evenings or the bridge parties my aunt gave about three or four times during the winter in our old family mansion in town, either because the fact that she rented out rooms in her villa was regarded as a comedown in social position, or because she was considered a poor bridge player, or else (though she belonged to a "good" set) because she did not share that exclusive passion for music which prevailed in our family, the question of Jewishness never having been mentioned, at least in my presence, even by allusion (contrary to the affair of the thousand-legger, which my mother made into a lasting grievance) in that nonetheless ultra-Catholic and reactionary milieu, either because it was felt to be in bad taste or else, as seems likely, because it was not current in that extreme southern part of France where many Marranos from the neighboring country had settled, so that for a long time I never knew that the blue-painted sign of the little dry-goods shop which stood at the corner of our street and of which a handwritten version could also be seen among other advertisements on the movie-house curtain during intermission, "Chez Sam: Notions" should have read: "Chez Samuel," etc. . . . .

The other occupant of the double room into which my bed was rolled after that first night spent in TRANSIT 2 was an old man about whom the first thing that struck me (as if the memory of the stump-men and of my mother associated with suffering and death the image of those beaklike noses whose diminution caused by disease and by age ended by making them, to the detriment of all other features, the chief element of a face) was one of those prominent and so to speak knife-edged noses which seem to have erased any other feature, along with, as another striking element, a long silvery mane of hair combed back to curl over the nape of his neck and which as I made my entrance he was in the process of combing with great care, sitting up in his bed, wearing bright red velour pajamas and a navy blue bathrobe, not stopping to respond to my greeting (or at least so it seemed to me), continuing to comb and smooth what for him appeared to constitute a sort of precious and ornamental helmet.

I never understood (the property was only four kilometers from the sea, and from the terrace you could see that blue stripe on the horizon) for what reasons (except perhaps to please the children) my aunt and her husband had come here for the summer, renting that huge and hideous villa which not only by its size but even by its esthetics (built on the shores of the Mediterranean in an incongruous Norman style and topped off with an overhanging roof that looked just like a bonnet) contrasted, pretentious, heavy and foreign-looking as it was, with the modest little pavilions like the one in which Maman had rented from that Madame Espinosa those two uncomfortable rooms daubed with a pink that had already faded with the seaside humidity which also, rising by osmosis from the soil, darkened the walls at the bottom, turning pink to mauve, as was evident when the bed had to be pulled out from the wall where the crazed thousand-legger had dropped to the floor and where the light from the candle Maman was holding to help in the creature's pursuit while uttering shrieks of terror mingled with in-dignation with regard to Madame Espinosa, revealing the crumbling, grainy and pale gray, of the salt-saturated plaster in which, coming loose in flakes under the clumsy blows meant for our quarry, shimmered tiny crystals of quartz.

In any case, and however paradoxical the matter might seem, since only a hundred yards separated the sea from the villa built right on the beach, my aunt's husband lost no opportunity to oversee the construction, halfway across the beach, of a traditional shelter, the sea breeze flapping its pink-striped canvas curtains, faded not so much from the humidity as from the sun which devoured their color until gradually it appeared as no more than a faint shadow on the grainy texture of the material. A shelter which, as night fell, rid of its canvas drapery and the visiting ladies who had their "salon" in the afternoons, sitting on folding chairs and wearing if not town clothes at least the most conservative summer dresses, perhaps permitting themselves, though still wearing their stockings, to slip on espadrilles—just as it would never have occurred to my aunt, still a comparatively young woman, to put on a bathing suit, however capacious, and an old yellowed photograph displays, sitting at the water's edge on a deck chair, wearing a huge hat and swathed in veils, like a heap of rags shaded by a parasol, my grandmother beside whom can be seen some young children (one of whom was almost a young man) wearing bathing suits with sleeves to the elbow, striped (pink?) horizontally and carefully buttoned down the front from neck to crotch . . .

A shelter, then, which at nightfall, rid of its removable curtains and reduced to a mere carcass, served as a rendezvous for a little group of children whose naive games, riddles or quizzes, occupied the time before going, under the supervision of some servant or other, to watch what was called the "trolling," i.e., a little to the north of the villas, upon the return of the fishing boats, the spectacle of women, young people and even children hauling up onto the beach the two ends of a huge net in which, by lantern light, could eventually be seen the bulging pouch in which a silvery mass of fish throbbed in chaotic desperation.

Yet for the little boy I was, more than this spectacle itself: the black water lapping faintly at big boats tipping from side to side near the beach, the line of haulers (women in black scarves or hatless, children more or less in tatters, men with their knotty and hairy feet) whose faces, lit from underneath by the lanterns set on the sand, inverting the shadows, acquired that mysterious and sacred quality which, in paintings or catechism illustrations representing the Nativity, transforms and magnifies the shepherds who have gathered around, illuminated by the light emanating from the manger, and last of all what seemed the enormous mass of quivering silver which filled the pouch of the net, everything combining to give the scene a sort of biblical and somehow fabulous dimension like the Miraculous Draught of Fishes or the Miracle of the Loaves and Fishes . . .

But more than the magical characteristics of this spectacle, what for me constituted the real virtue of those nocturnal experiences on the beach was the existence in our little group of a girl (she might have been about thirteen) who had assumed the leadership among us, haloed in my eyes (and doubtless in those of the other children as well) with the glamor that she derived from her noisy entrance on stage in a little play adapted, I think, by our English prof from some novel or other and put on for a party at the Cours Maintenon where my little cousin was enrolled, and in the course of which, disguised as a boy and wearing a cap, she burst on stage coming to someone's rescue, leaping into the center of a London slum through a window which as I remember was set stage right, as I can still hear the muffled sound of the floorboards under the shock of her feet and see the faint cloud of dust that rose up from them.

Either because she had been selected for the part precisely because of her vivacity and her boyish manners, or because the part influenced her behavior, she had gained an ascendancy over our little group which I accepted with mute but no less impassioned fervor into which, given my age (I must have been about five or six years old at the time), there entered no explicit sexual dimension but which was nonetheless so violent that many years later the memory of her noisy and rescuing entrance on stage still figures so vividly that I still seem to hear that noise of her landing on the floorboards, subsequently fastening the image onto that of the leap made by Andrée, Albertine's chum, over the "poor old guy" sitting on the promenade at Balbec.

Perhaps it was the effect of that fever which seemed to interpose a sort of screen between the external world and myself (affecting to the same degree my visual faculties), or perhaps it was simply the fact that this room in which I was quartered with the bony-faced old man was rather dim (overlooking some narrow inner courtyard, or else too close to another building?), for later on, once I had been taken to a new one (the private room), everything seemed suddenly flooded with light (an impression that might have been due to the relief of being alone now in addition to a notable lowering of the fever), but, during those first two days in the company of the sick old man, everything (including the likelihood of death implied not only by the doctors' serious faces but by the complicated apparatus attached to me) had seemed submerged in a sort of wan (even dark) gray, as in that painting beside the entrance to the Musée Dupuytren at the fair, an exhibition tent upon which we cast longing glances and about which it was rumored (children were not allowed inside) that the exhibits included, among other curiosities, skeletons, fetuses of various ages stuffed in jars of formaldehyde, and above a slit in the tent giving access to a sort of inner chamber, the inscription "Mysteries of Woman"—a painting more than faded, its colors quite washed out (so that the cardboard backing, apparently much folded in the course of being transported so often, revealed in several places, bordered by tiny flakes of dried paint, a number of star-shaped creases in the canvas), considered alluring both by the "scientific" seriousness of the scene represented and, one might assume, by the fact that it proposed the spectacle of a half-naked woman whose flung-back blouse revealed an expanse of grayish flesh while one of the figures beside her (Charcot? Pasteur? . . .), sitting on a chair, wearing a surgeon's toque and, over his suit, a sort of apron of the kind worn by cobblers (although white), pointed at a place between the bared breasts of the woman accompanied by two nuns in starched coifs; the scene doubtless historical but having become in this manner, on the canvas wall of a tent lit by an acetylene lamp, somehow emblematic, the secular affirmation (despite the presence of the two nuns) overriding all taboos (including that of nudity, as revealed by this bare-breasted woman in the presence of a circle of gentlemen in hats, neckties and gloves), social as well as scientific, as indicated by the expressions of the faces or the astonished gestures of some of the spectators.

. . .

As for that much-despised "Society Beach" and the humble attempts of the dance-hall music wafting from it to contend with the sound of the waves which immediately smothered it, I was to recall them many years later, on the very eve of the war, lying on the deck of one of those huge boats (not the ones that in my childhood were used for "trolling"—a kind of fishing so unlikely to be profitable that I think it has long since been abandoned—but equipped for sardine fishing and working out of some port on the rocky coast) anchored offshore for the night, when a strong land breeze came up, overcoming the sea wind which had blown all day, beginning by covering the sea's surface with a reticulation of tiny wavelets running in the opposite direction from the long swell which was very slow to settle—and the silence and only the occasional rustle, here or there, of one of those wavelets, its crest breaking so that the setting sun cast bronze patches on the no longer blue but bottle-green water darkening now, finally black in the black silence so that I could no longer make out the deck except by the faint reddish glow of a lantern, the boat pitching gently at anchor, the black thrust of the mast pointing up into the sky, swaying lazily from one constellation to the next, sometimes abruptly righted or skewed by a stronger wave, then resuming its indolent oscillation, the faint lapping and nothing else, when suddenly (this happened not gradually but all at once) the air (by which I mean its substance, its composition) changed: becoming a little thicker, somehow opaque after the transparent purity of the sea breeze giving way to it, not very strong at first, then asserting itself, laden not only with the heavy land smells which the scorching August sun had been stewing all day (smells of mown hay, of farm animals, of smoke), but also with that uncertain quantity of sounds, that vast vaguely familiar and vaguely disturbing murmur from which now and then emerged the barking of dogs or the whistles of locomotives and, in gusts, tenuous but quite distinct in spite of the distance, mingling with the faint nocturnal whispering of the sea, borne by the wind from the slender chaplet of lights flickering along the low coast, the brassy or velvety bursts of dance-hall music including one from the imposing casino which had recently replaced the yellow cement cube to which the tarred sheds of Society Beach had given way.

It is difficult to understand why, tormented by jealousy, the narrator (who, as Proust suggests, might be named Marcel) entrusts Albertine each afternoon to that Andrée whom (after Cottard's remark about the two girls dancing together at the Petit Casino) he suspects of enjoying with his mistress a "special" or rather a Gomorrhean friendship: a word rather unfortunately coined in order to avoid "Lesbian" (and perhaps to constitute a poetic pendant to "Sodomite"), phonetically suggesting as it does *logorrhea* or even *gonococcus*. Though of course problems of verisimilitude do not trouble Marcel Proust who, when necessary, resorts quite shamelessly to the most shopworn methods (such as accidents, coincidences, fortuity: for example, when he "involuntarily" observes the famous first encounter of Jupien and Charlus, or again, when, "exhausted" he enters—again "by accident" and "to rest a little"—the male brothel kept by Jupien and "surprises" the innocent remarks exchanged by the whip-wielding false Apaches.

The reader is similarly astonished, to say the least, by the dramatic accounting of certain practices the same narrator produces at the beginning of *Sodom and Gomorrha*, the accursed adepts of which he presents at great length before informing the reader that these "accursed" persons are to be numbered in the thousands in every society and that the barons, counts or dukes among his acquaintances bragged to each other about the charms and valor of their splendid footmen. And, as in the case of anti-Semitism, I do not recall, in the course of my childhood and in the most straitlaced milieu of my upbringing, having heard the slightest condemnation of such practices of which the most visible representative himself belonged to what was considered (or considered itself) the "society" (though, in his case, a trifle tarnished) of the town, a man already of a certain age who called himself a poet and whose narrative of such escapades trumpeted with great self-satisfaction constituted the fabric of universal gossip, his identity as a poet justified by a monthly page which he composed with the help of friends and of several poetesses, laureates of the "Golden Gorse" in the Floral Games of Toulouse, especially prized for the main column which he permitted no one else to compose. As for his own exploits our "society" marveled at, the two chief ones— at least for as long as I lived in the place—were first, a nocturnal bacchanale on the grounds of the Grand Hotel of a nearby spa, unfortunately interrupted by the arrival of the police who had been alerted by the hotel manager (or the head chef), concerned about the absence of a young scullion, and second a flattering proposition made in the Turkish baths of the same spa (which appeared to be his favorite hunting grounds) by an Eastern potentate to take advantage of a fortunate temporary erection, a word (erection) which, probably on a dare, one of my grown-up cousins, though known for her extreme prudishness and her extreme piety, repeated several times with the somewhat masculine (and also somewhat aggressive) assurance she had acquired from a training period at her diocesan dispensary where, she declared with the same aggressivity, it was only natural to provide care, "as well," for the unfortunate victims of venereal disease. At best, the town (its "society"—and the most respectable portions thereof) regarded this "poet" in its midst (a situation which already constituted a certain guarantee) with deferential respect for his qualities as a wit (which his qualities as an invert managed to confirm by virtue of that belief—or rather axiom—that talent and pederasty (or the reverse) are necessarily complementary), as indeed a somewhat clownish element but suited to foster its intellectual chronicle and in a certain sense indispensable to any "structured" society.

Sardines were fished offshore from a little harbor at sunset and at sunrise, the nets set perpendicular to the line bisecting the angle formed by the tide and the setting (or rising) sun, which in a picturesque phrase the fishermen expressed by saying that they always worked "with one eye on the tide and the other on the setting—or rising—sun." If the evening or "prime" catch was big enough, the boat returned to the harbor where the auction managers were waiting. If the catch was judged too small to cover the cost of fuel, the boat was anchored offshore, gently rocking (while the sailors stretched out on deck until just before dawn), and then those magical nights began.

The old man (my neighbor in the double room where I was taken immediately after that first night in TRANSIT

1) the very first sight of whom gave me a shock, an immediate and insurmountable shudder of repulsion, not that the poor wretch was dirty or nauseating, but perhaps, paradoxically, because his person seemed to incarnate to the point of caricature a somehow obscene resistance to what the two of us were there for, as if I had been allowed to see and cohabit with a sort of sneering double of myself, by which I mean that awful will the old man showed not only to live but to deny a collapse which he incarnated to an unendurable degree, constantly passing that little comb back and forth through his long silvery head of hair which itself seemed of a beauty and an elegance quite contrary to the blighted countenance of the pathetic old creature on whose skull it gleamed like an artificial accessory, like that wig with frozen waves which not out of coquetry of course but rather out of a concern for decency (and doubtless to spare me a vision that would be too alarming) Maman (I learned later on) persisted in wearing—at least until the day when I saw her for the last time—framing a similar and tragic countenance of some bird of prey, as if I was condemned to see of death, at least of the death which is called "natural" (or at least of its approach) only that grotesque and macabre puppet show (reminding me of that prisoner the Germans had paraded through the whole camp, attached to a leash held by two others ordered to walk very slowly and wearing on his chest, hanging round his neck by a wire, a heavy brick (or a stone?) on which was written "I stole my com-

rades' bread," and who, after all the insults, wads of spit, and sometimes blows, had acquired the same look by the time he had passed through our barracks, the same flesh- less, collapsed and terrifying aspect of an old man on the verge of death). The old and so to speak Goyaesque man, then, whose insistent coquetry was not confined to comb- ing his hair but also involved his garments, those theat- rically scarlet pajamas over which, with the nurse's help, he pulled the elegant navy blue bathrobe before dragging himself very slowly to the bathroom we shared where I was afterwards disgusted to find, although (or perhaps because) they were so carefully arranged, his comb, tooth- brush and nailbrush, the sticky pink cake of soap, and two bath towels, the kind sold in open-air markets, printed with fruit, leaves, and blossoms in a washed-out symphony of orange, green, and a color which was not pink but somehow a senility of red. But what was more appalling than all the rest (more than the horror of his soap, of his comb, of his toothbrush and the evanescent mildewed colors of his bath towels still somehow impreg- nated with their contact with a body which old age and exhaustion had not so much emaciated as rendered unfit to live), was the way in which that will to endure was made manifest against all reason and one might have said against all decency, sparing gestures and movements in a way that had something terrifying about it, each gesture, each movement seeming to be its own caricature, not that he stumbled or came close to falling or miscalculated his gestures: quite the contrary, these gestures participated in a watchful economy (not to say avarice) of his strength, but he conducted them (there is no other word for it) with such deliberation that his every movement, his slightest action, assumed a sort of hallucinatory quality— and yet not the kind that can be seen in a film projected in slow motion (where the very stumbles, the blows (horses, boxers, jockeys, soccer players) have a sort of airy grace, resilient and so unreal that the spectator immediately realizes that this is a slowing-down of normal movements shown, so to speak, in weightlessness), but on the contrary of a heavy slowness, in which the laws of weight never lost their powers but from which there resulted no stumbles, no trembling, and no clumsiness: the slightest movement led and guided so to speak from initiation to conclusion with a minute solicitude which made him successively turn back the sheets, sit up in his bed, gradually slide to the floor, pull the bathrobe over the hideous red velour pajamas, knotting the belt with a number of precautions in which were concentrated and then carefully distributed all his will, all his attention, and all his powers, conducted with great precaution in their most insignificant phases, as if not something alive but a mechanism (a mechanism of extreme precision) were controlling them, entirely without those abrupt shocks which jolt the limbs of automata: each movement of his body linking with something which was in a sense the opposite of grace and which made this whole spectacle even more hallucinatory, as if ever since I had come into the emergency ward (but once again, was this the effect of the fever?) there extended before me a sequence of events, or of bizarre manifestations of life (or of a sort of enchanted, secret world suddenly revealed) from the clownish drunkard to this sort of geared-down activity of the old man, and between them the enigmatic severed head with the blond hair as motionless as a wax mask in the center of its ace of diamonds. Now, from a needle stuck in my wrist and kept there by a square of adhesive tape, a tube ran to a sort of bladder made of a whitish substance which gradually wrinkled as it hung from a sort of gibbet furnished with a crown of hooks at the top of a long chromium stem, and if I still had two oxygen tubes in my nostrils, at least I was rid of that blood-pressure bracelet which automatically contracted and relaxed at fixed intervals the first night; yet I still saw everything in monochrome in the dim gray light of that room, except for the old man in his garish pajamas who moved with such prudent, precise and scrupulous deliberation—and although, since I had been put in that room, both of us, as if by a tacit agreement as to the uselessness (or the futility) of speaking, had kept silence, he now murmured in my direction, with a sort of disabused smile, some unintelligible words which were doubtless meant to be friendly since he pressed a switch somewhere that turned on the screen rather high up on the wall facing the two beds, and on the screen appeared against a pale green background a cluster of tiny men

running after a ball, but I must have made a gesture or
something like a face for he immediately turned it off with
a similar gesture or expression of annoyance and then,
still with that same fascinating economy of movements,
sat up on the edge of his bed, taking his little comb out
of his breast pocket and passing it several times through
his silver hair, then putting it back, leaning his torso to
one side, disengaging one sleeve of his bathrobe, then the
other, pulling it out from under his buttocks, then pivoting on them and sliding his legs under the sheet, and
finally, his ruined countenance still impassive, staring
wide-eyed at the ceiling, becoming absolutely motionless.

. . . Only when I came back for the summer vacation the
chaise longue was no longer there I remember that without saying a word I went looking for it first in that bed
room or rather that salon in the right wing which opened
onto the garden by two French doors and which had been
made into a bedroom for her so that it could be pushed
outside easily lying on the chaise longue covered with that
cretonne embroidered with tiny bouquets and narrow
pink stripes, not some kind of garden furniture made out
of bamboo or rattan but a solid piece with carved (eb-
ony?) feet attached to pivoting wheels that were quite un-
serviceable on the gravel so that it had to be carried
outside her body lying on top of it reduced to a bundle

of bones inside a withered skin which didn't add much weight but which it still took two people to move in order to keep it in the shade of those trees whose exact name I don't know part cypress part cedar the leaves a sort of mournful dark green if you could call them leaves those tiny spindles like fishbones no larger than the little twig-like leaves that species of conifer has but I couldn't find it anywhere wondering if to keep me from seeing it they had sold it or burned it or chopped it to pieces with an axe and tossed it on the compost heap near the pine grove and I even looked there without seeming to do so to see if I could discover the pieces but found nothing Now I was sleeping in the bedroom just overhead the corner room in the right wing of the building so that when I was sent up to bed tearing me away from the contemplation of the bridge game my cousins ritually played by the light of that big copper oil lamp and the wick had to be constantly watched because it easily smoked and charred, or from those musical evenings during which one of my cousins accompanied by my aunt at the piano sang those *lieder* or *mélodies* Schubert Chausson Duparc *Der Erlkönig*, which my oldest cousin who had been a student at Krefeld used to sing in German *Mein Vater! Mein Vater!* . . . each cry empha-sized by low trills in the bass notes of the piano sug-gesting thunderstorms or else that *Invitation au Voyage* singing *Mon enfant ma soeur* and so on after which some-one would say Now children It's time (or It's late) and to get from the left wing to the right I would have to cross the garden shielding the candle constantly threatening to blow out then pulling open the screen door the bottom of which scraped loudly against the doorsill and sometimes jammed and the washer of the handle would come loose the upper part banging against the jamb, then making my way into the dark entrance hall then climbing the dark winding staircase the walls papered if I remember right with an ugly pattern of vertical olive-green and garnet stripes made of imitation plush between thin gold threads then crossing the tiled landing to my bedroom opening the door and releasing each time a gust of air which bent the candle flame almost horizontal but I could have made my way without any light into that bedroom with its wallpaper of huge poppies their hairy stems twisting upwards against a greenish-gray background.

Sometimes it was the maid who first caught sight of it in the morning as she was hanging out the laundry to dry in the attic and shouted to me to leave my breakfast (that hot chocolate *à l'espagnole*, without milk, so that the little spoon would stand straight up in it, the way Maman had grown used to it as a girl in Barcelona and which my loathing of milk had got me in the habit of drinking), then snatching up my satchel, running across the garden and down the path lined with mulberry bushes, head turned to the left, eyes following the trolley which was rapidly approaching, all that I could see at first above the scarlet or pink autumn vines would be the big Nouvelles Galeries sign running along the roof on one side, then the whole car itself visible, moving fast, then slowing down, stopping finally at the foot of the big umbrella pine which marked the end of the path where two or three women carrying baskets were usually waiting whom I let climb in first and sit down on the benches inside the car while I remained standing in that privileged place in the conductor's cab.

(You could see that the network of tiny waves stirred at twilight by the land breeze did not oppose the offshore swell merely running on the surface or rather the skin of the sea climbing the shifting crests slipping back down into the troughs like the assault waves of a lilliputian army invading a hilly region Occasionally a stronger swell lifted the heavy boat which fell back with a slap spreading a sheet of clawed foam on one side which collapsed in a shower of chilly droplets the sound quite audible when they scattered over the sea's surface Near me from time to time passed a man on watch crossing the deck for some task or other his bare feet just discernible in the half-darkness but so present to me however furtive (seeming quite close to my face then vanishing immediately swallowed up by the shadows) that they might have belonged to some marine divinity not so much muscular as gnarled corroded by salt edged by bright-pink calluses and ending in ridged yellowish toenails roughly squared off both feet somehow animated with a life of their own beneath the body of some invisible giant who as in those drawings by Granville might have belonged to a fish or at least had a fish's head, able at the same time to feel underneath me that powerful thing gently lifting the big boat then receiving it gently as in a liquid cradle then rising once again)

Beginning to run in hopes of catching that fateful trolley once I had closed the classroom door behind me, rushing down the stairs, across the courtyards, coming out on that courthouse square which was in a sense the center of the modern town at the heart of which once used to face each other, testifying to an ancient past, the old Gothic market and what was called "Le Cercle" (the provincial and old-fashioned equivalent of that famous Parisian Jockey Club of which one member proclaimed Thanks be to God there are still some of us here who owe nothing to either merit or talent) where gossip alleged that "fortunes" were gambled away every night and on the long balcony of which could be seen, during the day, leaning on the banister or swaying in rockers, the solemn gentlemen with white moustaches supposed, after dark, to hold the cards in their wrinkled hands, surrounded by those young people or at least young mistresses whom, in their jargon, the older boys at school called *les poules* (most of them, people said, daughters of their tenant farmers or of their stewards—or else just grape-pickers chosen from the seasonal troupes of gypsies, hastily cleaned up, taught to read and write, and covered with flashy jewelry), the word itself (*poule*), by its circular morphology (like *boule*) and then too doubtless from a combination of images mingling such girls with the dance-hall hostesses sashaying through "saloons" in the movies and, strangely enough, the members' wives with their tearful voices and their overflowing flesh who used to visit my grandmother, so that to my imagination they evoked those opulent creatures I could see sketched in the newspapers, their creamy breasts bursting out of corsets so tightly laced they suggested horns of plenty brimming over with fruits (or some peculiar sort of ice-cream cones), vaunting the mammary efficacity of rival products, such as Oriental Lozenges or Kala Busta Salve. As for the old gentlemen themselves (who more likely than gambling away the whispered "fortunes" attempted to distract themselves by a few miserly hands of whist—or simply of écarté), though for me they all had the face of my uncle, the widower of my oldest aunt, himself the descendant, like my grandmother, of a Napoleonic general (though belonging to a corps (Quartermaster) regarded as inglorious, drowned moreover with no special martial dis-

tinction while crossing the Berezina) and whom (the old
gentleman, her son-in-law) she (my grandmother) held responsible for her daughter's death, as they described it in
those days, "of a consumption of the breast," blaming him
for having brutally exposed her to the rigors of a winter in
an Eastern garrison town (Lunéville, Toul?) where, according to a family tradition, he had (before, according to the
same tradition, submitting his resignation for "personal
reasons") served a while as a cavalry or artillery officer, I no
longer know which: the latter seeming more likely, that service implying a certain disposition for the sciences or the
technologies which seemed to have been exercised (expressed) in his passion for puttering, dedicating to this
occupation the hours he failed to spend at Le Cercle, tin-
kering with the sort of maritime engineering which led
him to accumulate in his attic, transformed into a work-
shop and furnished with the most modern equipment
(electric lathes, stamping-press, soldering irons, etc.), a
veritable fleet of scale models ranging from steamer and
battleship to simple fishing ketch, including the picturesque side-wheeler we could see in the movies chugging
up and down the Mississippi, priding himself on the tiny
artisanal masterpiece also fabricated by himself which
consisted of a moustache-shield which he first waved under my grandmother's nose before tying the strings behind his head and attacking the ritual soup, the family
condemned to listen, as course followed course, to the
nasal and self-satisfied monologue he produced on every

conceivable subject: describing the no-trump (or the grand slam) which he had, the day before (or two months previously: although his descriptions never failed, the actual events in his life seemed rather infrequent), cleverly made at Le Cercle (with many specific details as to the hands in which the jack of clubs or the queen of hearts were the highest card, the lessons in mechanics he had given to his chauffeur, or even—an episode from which he appeared to derive a particular delight, if not even a certain pride, and which he called a "capital execution"— the firing of some tenant farmer or steward) the two old people (although son-in-law and mother-in-law, they seemed to our children's eyes to belong to the same generation) forming under the harsh (actually, rather cruel) light of the dining-room chandelier which revealed and in fact exposed their shrunken mask-like countenances (and, in our grandmother's case, ravaged as well), a fantastic couple (he with his face barred as though by a wound-dressing by that moustache-shield which seemed to be concealing some horrible scar—as if he had received a horizontal saber slash full in the face, she with that eternal grimace of a Greek mask of tragedy), as though emerging from the depths of time, or rather of History, for whatever the horror in which the pious old lady might have held her own ancestor, alas a member of the Convention and a regicide even before the Empire, she nonetheless kept in her salon his marble bust with its shoulders draped in a toga, its frowning brows, and its leonine mane, beside which the wan memory of a General in the Quartermaster Corps drifting among the ice floes of the Berezina counted, after all, for very little—which did not keep the old lady from regarding it as her duty to her late daughter, in spite of her repugnance, to invite the widowed husband to these biannual ceremonial feasts, on which occasions she disinterred her best wines to accompany the interminable and lugubrious celebrations which alas he regularly and punctually attended. As for the town, it was as if it had repudiated itself (repudiating its royal church, the palace where Charles V had slept, its fortress, the ramparts with which Vauban himself had subsequently surrounded it), so to speak exploding, blossoming, acceding (at the ends of its narrow medieval streets) to a sort of antithesis of itself under the aspects of a modernity moreover almost immediately deteriorated, already dated and fragile, in which, by an alloy of faith in Progress as in the classical canons, were paradoxically combined, around the conquered esplanade on a demolished section of the ancient ramparts: the statue of a dignitary in a bronze frock coat, the courthouse façade in the form of a Corinthian temple, the new branch of the Crédit Lyonnais, and, under the sign of D. GOUGOL, CAFÉ-GLACIER, the massive iron and glass rotonda patterned after a miniature Gallery of Mechanical Inventions and also a bandstand where, close as the town is to Spain, a Gypsy orchestra played waltzes from Viennese operettas and the last refrains of the Belle Époque, modernizations (or transformations, or embellishments) which had apparently been brought about (like a butterfly spasmodically extracting itself from its chrysalis and at last spreading its iridescent wings) in four phases to which we owed first of all the Corinthian temple, then the bronze statue, then the wondrous dragonfly, the masterpiece of iron and glass, and ultimately, in a fourth and final effort, the rococo façade of the movie-palace where the trolley reached the end of the line.

That maid (to use, for lack of others ("servant" sounds pompous) this word with all it implies (of servility, of submission, of humiliation, of abuse ("of all work"), of scornful indulgence) . . . that maid, then, who worked for Maman (calling the boy I was "Monsieur") and who took care of her to the end with all this word (care) also implies concerning actions not strictly medical (injections, dressings, potions) but distasteful; such as washing that excessively white, almost skeletal body, setting it on the bedpan, wiping it, disposing of its evacuations, changing the drawsheets (once having come into her bedroom without warning and made to leave, as if I had surprised some rite, some vaguely obscene, clandestine, or sacred ceremony, like some illegal entombment). Always dressed in black, bending over the livid body her impassive, indecipherable countenance which she always presented un-

changed, whether serving at table or killing a chicken, not
bony but somehow long and sharpened, as if carved out
of some inert yellow substance, permanently stamped
with an expression of mute indignation, as if the whole
world were the reason for a sort of continual aggression
to which she reacted in the identical fashion, at once sub-
missive and enraged, whether to change soiled sheets or,
as was her custom, to burn alive in their cage over the
high flames of the stove the rats caught in her traps, indifferent to (or pleased with?) their horrible writhing, actually inviting us children to observe this dreadful
spectacle, as if it were an act of both disinfection and
justice, when it was over dropping into the garbage the
charred remains of these wretched creatures in the same
way she threw out potato peels or chicken heads: as if
Maman and she formed a sort of inseparable couple
linked by a common knowledge of misery, the one (Maman) struggling (but did she struggle?—or was she only
waiting for it to come to an end? submitting to the doctors' prescriptions, for instance those pellets of raw meat,
only out of a sense of duty or perhaps a proud thirst for
martyrdom?) . . . struggling against death, then, the other
one (the maid) like (with that narrow, desiccated face
framed by two locks of hair escaping from her bun, her
rheumy eyes, her gaping fish-mouth, her slight limp, her
eternal black clothes) that figure in a painting by Breughel
(or Hieronymus Bosch? . . .) armed with a scythe and
striding through a landscape strewn with corpses, age-

less—at least to my eyes—not only during the time she spent in Maman's service but even later, when after Maman's death she went to work for my aunt, like those domestic animals, racing dogs or saddle horses, which members of the same family transfer to each other's possession, not so much with the assurance that the successor will take care of them: rather as if what was involved was not a matter of a different social class but of a sort of caste—of untouchables—nor could I remember (except for the twice-folded banknote my aunt put in my hand when I went to say goodbye to her at the end of vacation) any sort of behavior on the part of some member of the family which might have betrayed some feeling of affection for her, maybe something like esteem, maybe too something like a sort of condescending assistance, as for instance, when at her brother's death (for she had a brother, a creature as mysterious and ageless as herself who used to visit her once or twice a year and whom she would ask permission to give lunch to in the kitchen, glimpsed there in a shadowy corner, cadaverous too and glum (not humble: glum), rising timidly from his chair if you came in, lifting a cap to revealed a bald and livid skull, then disappearing for months) . . . when at this brother's death, then, she indicated a desire to go to the village where she and her brother had grown up to settle (or to find) some business, my aunt's husband drove her, taking us with him, to a hamlet, if you could give such a name to the gathering of several more or less dilapidated houses (not even, as you can still see in mountainous regions, stone cabins smeared with rough mortar and roofed with machine-made tiles) on the stony mountainside (almost at the height where, in early autumn, you can see the first snows from the plain below), the (so to speak, hamlet?) apparently deserted, although at this hour of the day you might have thought the men were in the fields (but there were no fields: only stones), except for three women, they too dressed in black, standing on a doorstep, staring into the distance without moving, and in the middle of the road a bony gray donkey standing in a cloud of tiny midges clustered around its eyes and a bright-red wound on its withers and refusing to move when my aunt's husband, getting out of the car, tried to shoo it off the road, still standing there, as motionless as if it were made of stone, until she got out in her turn, walked toward it, said some words at the same time that she gave it a slap (just one) on the neck, whereupon it walked away quite unconcernedly, some of the midges sucking the red wound flying up, surrounding the open car, landing on our faces, especially our lips, impossible to brush off, and while waiting for her to come back my aunt's husband turned the car around on the flattened summit of a pile of debris, in front of the entrance, on the hillside, to what had been an iron mine, now abandoned, all that remained being a line of pylons supporting slack cables to which were attached, hanging askew over the void and swaying faintly in the wind—in the sky where an eagle soared in wide circles, motionless, wings outspread—several rusty shaft-buckets.

The body of the trolley was about seven meters long, the front and rear parts through which you entered and where there was a motorman's cab at either end, were made of steel plates and painted yellow, the central part where the passengers sat on two wooden benches facing one another was covered outside with vertical wooden struts stained brown. Above the windows ran those two long advertisements which framed the car like two ears, the one on the right consisting of the sign for the Nouvelles Galeries, the one on the left vaunting the merits of Eclipse Wax (or was it a brand of some kind of pasta?—I no longer remember) where, at one end, a smiling full moon concealed three-quarters of a tearful sun, advertisements which were to be seen in various places around town with no respect for the buildings or even the monuments on which they were posted, the most frequent being those for "SUZE—*apéritif à la gentiane*," the name SUZE in monumental yellow letters shaded in black on an olive-green background, the garish colors now dimmed by time and a certain patina, blending attractively into a sort of uniform gray, and concurrently BYRRH, in letters just as monumental but white (and in the same kind of false relief) on a pink background; these might be called wild

advertisements, escaping regulation (or tolerated in return for some payment under the table—the manufac-
turers of this rival aperitif, being purchasers of enormous
quantities of wine throughout the region, constituting a
veritable and virtually feudal local power), simultaneously
aggressive and amusingly naive (like those faces of smiling
or tearful heavenly bodies), posted—along with others—
as often on the town hall's Renaissance arcades as on the
nearby walls of apartment buildings, giving the center of
town not a brand-new but a comically gaudy appearance
matching the somewhat old-fashioned style of the advertisements which, aside from those promoting Oriental
Lozenges, could be seen in the local newspapers, for instance that impassive (or even smiling) countenance of a
man with a moustache holding a hammer and pounding
on a piece of iron like the kind used by blacksmiths to
split a tree trunk, the iron already disappearing into his
skull, the whole design bearing the caption "Get this into
your head," or another man, he too with a moustache,
wearing nothing but tights, bent double, one of his arms
curved back and one hand set on his hip in a position so
expressive that there was no need to read the caption promoting a miraculous unguent for back pains. No adver-
tisement, on the other hand, framed the roof of the trailer
called *la baladeuse* attached in summertime to the trolley
and which on the August 15 holidays (when for three days
it was an unwritten law that no member of the family
(nor any of our connections—the roomers in the villas

or their owners then returning to town) was to be seen on the beach, traditionally invaded on the occasion of these celebrations by the habitués of Society Beach who then overflowed the plank enclosure in which they were habitually confined), days when in the blinding almost colorless summer light we could see the cars passing every ten minutes (the Trolley Company on this occasion quadrupling the schedules), towing these open-air trailers from which, as the canvas curtains fluttered like wings in the wind of their passage, escaped the screams or the songs of a crowd already quite drunk or simply having a good time, sporadic echoes, at first remote, then growing louder, exploding when the trolley passed at the far end of the Allée des Mûriers, then gradually growing fainter before dying away between the pines, the dusty laurels, and the iris-bordered beds in the garden where lying like a sort of fan on that chaise longue covered with flowered cretonne, which was shifted on the gravel according to the position of the sun and the resulting shade, Maman was slowly dying.

And it was the same the following summer, except that Maman was no longer there and during the month of October I no longer had to run to catch that four o'clock trolley, having already returned to my school in Paris, which freed me from participating in the traditional autumn move which brought the family to town and from having to listen to the traditional lamentations of my aunt whom this annual return plunged into an ostentatious collapse renewed each year when after four months in the country she found herself back in what she called her "tomb," i.e. the huge apartment which, though over-looking spacious courtyards and a spacious garden, was, it is true, darkened by the branches of a huge acacia tree; a return which, coinciding with All Saints' Day, was the annual pretext for my aunt (who had nonetheless been born there and had always lived there) to manifest that lofty despair sustained by a certain theatrical inclination which both sisters, Maman and she, seemed to inherit from our grandmother (apart from those lugubrious meals with the widower of her eldest daughter on which occasions she would invariably wear the same black silk blouse with vertical pleats, its starched front embroidered with glittering tubular (jet?) beads, its severe high collar that concealed the wattles of her neck invariably fastened with a mauve cameo) . . . grandmother whose tragic mask I still seem to see, supplanting all other images, floating weightless before me, livid and dusted with grayish powder, dark pouches beneath her eyes, her flesh pendulous and the corners of her mouth turned down, as though suspended in the void, somewhere in the labyrinth of dark corridors, stamped with an affliction mingled with lethargy, the very image of misfortune or rather of a sum of misfortunes including doubtless the loss of her husband (our grandfather) followed by that of her elder daughter, to which had then been added, though having a different impact but like an ultimate consummation, the necessity which the ravages of phylloxera and the slump in wine sales had forced upon her to sell one of the three properties she owned in the Département as well as one which she had inherited from her mother in the Gers, regarding herself thereafter as ruined despite the considerable fortune she still possessed which would, after her death, permit her eight grandchildren to live if not in luxury at least in comfort. An inclination, then, or a hereditary propensity to the theatrical which in my aunt (the dark gowns, the proud Bourbonian countenance with which, in an offended silence, she endured the affectionate teasing of my cousins) conferred upon this autumnal resurgence of a profound neurasthenia (or of some hidden frustration?) a sort of majesty which she abandoned only after two or three weeks, immediately sitting down at her piano with no transition at all, her face still impassive, haughty, and performing for herself with a sort of virile virtuosity one of those scores which, in those days, transposed into easy arrangements all the symphonies or overtures of the repertoire, favored as she was by an exceptional gift for sight-reading accompanied (or completed) by that no less prodigious memory which permitted her to declaim upon request the imprecations of Camille, the stanzas of the Cid, the *récit* of Théramène, or some other classical tirade, as well as to participate quite magisterially (forgetting neither a bid nor any card played) in those bridge tournaments which, along with musical evenings, constituted the rare social distractions in which that straitlaced provincial society allowed itself to engage (or so it appeared, for who would have believed that our cellist, daughter and niece of the two austere white-bearded music-loving bankers, would one day see her husband, himself an austere and exclusive music-lover, run off with a young secretary?), musical evenings of which the apotheosis, one year, was a performance of the César Franck quintet which, lacking among our friends the number of necessary talents, required inviting for the viola part (and not without, through all the rehearsals (for of course he was received on the evening of the great event itself with the utmost consideration), its being remarked upon with quite vulgar half-smiles) the best student from the Conservatory who happened to be the son of the hairdresser (the one who gave shampoos): the sonorous vibrations of the various stringed instruments accompanied (or heralded, or repeated, or thwarted) by the tripping notes of the piano, majestically swelling or diminishing into furtive murmurs under the scintillations of the crystal chandelier reflected in the heavy gilding of the frames around the fake Corots or the fake Daubignys acquired by the last male descendant of the fiery and jacobin general whose marble bust draped in Roman fashion seemed, with his frowning brows, his lumpy countenance and his leonine mane, a formidable challenge to the graceful head carved in a pale lardlike substance enthroned on the mantelpiece, coiffed with a tricorne like those worn by Watteau's marquises, the pupils grooved and fixed, the neck surrounded by a ribbon with a knot also carved in the same substance, obviously purchased on the honeymoon because it was Italy, because it was marble, and because that marble was from Carrara, so that it took my older cousins years of pleading to convince my aunt and her husband to relegate the thing to the attic.

That same long Erinye's face permanently stamped with an expression of outrage which she seemed never to leave off, whether caring for Maman with a sort of fierce tenderness or (suddenly appearing in the dim kitchen, leaning over the flickering glow of the flames) contemplating the torments of those rats she was burning alive (which, reported by the children, was strictly forbidden—despite which (but without witnesses) she doubtless continued doing), or again, still outraged and inflexible for all our pleading and tears, killing one after the other the kittens of her cat's incessant litters, flinging them violently against the courtyard wall, picking up the tiny sticky balls of bloody hair if they still moved, flinging them against the wall again and then dumping them on the compost heap out of a basket which she then rinsed several times until there was no trace of blood left in it.

·   ·   ·

The carts consisted of a thick wooden tray, about four meters long and one meter wide, resting on the axle which joined two big wheels the height of a man. The iron-bound wheels were usually painted pink, their spokes sometimes embellished with a slender yellow stripe which ended, near the rim, in a tiny stylized fleur-de-lys, these colors somewhat muted by the dust and very pale. The oval wooden tubs, filled to the brim with bunches of grapes, were set on the tray in pairs (five on each side), sometimes with two or three additional tubs on top. The tray was surrounded with iron stakes screwed into sockets at regular intervals in the broad iron belt around its edge, a chain running from stake to stake at the top, like the festoons of a garland. The carts were drawn by two strong Percherons harnessed one behind the other. Their withers supported a heavy leather collar, its conical top, curving backward, covered with a shiny brass plate. Following the lane of laurels separating the two gardens, the team entered the big courtyard and came to a halt when the cart was just below the opening in the cellar wall at the height of the planks covering the vats (replaced later on by cement troughs), each containing about two thousand liters. The first horse was then unhitched and slowly came forward so that there could be attached to its harness a long chain which, passing through a pulley over the cellar door, suspended at its other end, over the cart, an iron hook with two rings at each end which a man passed through the handles of a tub, after which he shouted

"*Amoun!*" (Up!) and the horse, advancing a few yards along the wall, pulled the chain which with a metallic rasping sound raised the tub to the level of the cellar door where, easily grabbing hold of it, two men pulled it onto the plank, one of them then shouting "*Abaïl!*" (Down!), the horse stepping backward to where it had been originally, and the hook, released, returning to its position above the cart. All the time the unloading lasted nothing could be heard in the garden but those two monotonous shouts, *Amoun, Abaïl,* coming from the courtyard at regular intervals and separated by the rasping noise of the chain in the pulley. Soon afterward the cart set off in the opposite direction loaded with the empty tubs, the driver now sitting sideways on the edge of the tray, his legs hanging down between the wheel and the beginning of the axle. Each tub contained around eighty kilograms of grapes, to which could be added its own weight of about fifteen kilograms. When they were full and at their maximum weight, as they were pulled up to the cellar door they knocked hard against the wall which was protected against just this occurrence by thick planks nailed vertically on either side. It also happened that one of the men receiving the tubs would now and then be seriously hurt. Since the men worked barefoot, their trouser-legs rolled halfway up their calves, one of them once had his foot crushed. I don't remember if it was Maman, still up and about in those days, or my cousin who was in training at the dispensary who dressed the wound, but, although someone was put in charge of taking the children away, I can still see that foot with its livid skin, all lumpy and rimmed with pink ochre, and the thick yellow toenails out of which ran a stream of blood, spiraling at first like smoke from a chimney, then completely reddening the water in the bowl while an almost childish cry emerged from the lips of the man being supported on a chair by two others.

The last trolley stop before that terminus where the rails vanished under the sand of the beach was about a kilometer from the end of the line, at a place where, to the right, framed by those silvery trees which grow in moist ground, there opened a long stony lane, it too half covered by sand; at the end of this lane appeared, not on a hill strictly speaking but at the top of what must have once been quite a high dune, a structure surrounded by pines and in an architectural style in favor during the Second Empire or at the beginning of the Third Republic, which is to say in imitation, on a reduced scale, of some chateau of the Loire which with its steeply sloping slate roof, its corner turrets, its mullioned windows, its imposing doorway at the top of a flight of steps, and its lawn with formal flowerbeds, paraded a wealth if not aristocratic (the name of its owners not being (and never having been) preceded by a particle) at least ostentatious despite the efforts of its present occupants, grandchildren of the man who, toward the end of the last century, had built the ambitious residence confining his offspring to that social sphere which envy—or resentment—surrounds with that simultaneously admiring and scornful aura manifested, for instance, in an undertone or an aside by certain jokes about the quality of the vineyards in the low, sandy fields which surrounded the place and constituted its wealth, producing, it was whispered, an abominable "ink" of just eight degrees, the extent and the yield by hectare of this derided vineyard being such, unfortunately for its detractors, that given an equal credit rating and even at the low price of such ink, it earned the inheritors of the absurd chateau five or six times more than one of those excellent hillside wines on which the detractors prided themselves, being eager moreover to respond to the invitations (afternoon teas, children's parties, or dinners) which were made three or four times each summer by these inheritors whose affability and good manners constituted the best argument against the supposed arrogance of the amateur of pseudo-Renaissance architecture, the shrewd purchaser of hundreds of easily-flooded hectares considered beneath contempt and acquired for almost nothing, one of them (one of these inheritors) supplying (like the pederastic poet, but on another level) grist for the town's scandal mills by rumors of certain escapades with women attributed to him along with certain imaginary losses in that Circle of perdition of which he was (or rather of which he had politely consented to be) one of the members (he

was not much over thirty) and where he appeared several
times, occasionally amusing himself by playing a few rub-
bers with the prudent old bridge-players at several francs
a point (those bridge games in which "fortunes" were
gambled . . .) like that son-in-law so hated by my grandmother (the descendant of the general drowned in the
Berezina and the builder of miniature fleets) and perhaps—if not quite probably—amusing himself as well
with the seduction of their *"poules"* despite the rather
friendly gossip (like the gossip concerning the homosex-
ual poet) which attributed to him (though always by in-
nuendo) this or that liaison with some married woman
of our "best society," adding this trump card to those
(fortune, youth, wit, charm, and inexhaustible good manners) which permitted him not only without being re-
proved but with a certain encouragement to utter in the
salons (half joking, half serious) the worst enormities
(verging for some on blasphemy) on various questions of
a social or religious or sexual order and which (like his
winnings at bridge or his paraded conquests) had perhaps
no other object than to create for himself a mask of amiable cynicism which concealed some secret melancholy
consoled by neither the absurd chateau nor the big automobile parked alongside the others belonging to his
family under the garage roof situated not far from the
lawn where the children invited to the summer parties
argued about their croquet matches; a car of some make
I no longer remember but which (like the ones belonging

to his mother or to his sisters) contrasted with the high-axled dull gray-green Ford which my aunt's husband parked a little farther away: an annual and quasi-ritual invitation supposed to abolish somehow the enormous gap yawning not only between the fortunes of the two families but even between their social positions, on one hand the heirs of the shrewd purchaser of the disdained vineyards with their phenomenal yields of ink and on the other their guests not exactly shabby-genteel but all the same, after all, obliged to consider . . . , each forgetting the respective advantages conferred on one hand by fortune and on the other by birth (or rather the prestige attached to it for all the same, after all, not forgetting the builder of the absurd chateau, the historic figure, member of the (moreover repudiated) Convention and Napoleonic general from whom the passengers in the Ford flattered themselves to be descended, already dated from a quite distant past), so that (but I knew no more than what a young boy can deduce from conversations abruptly broken off when he came into a room, or from certain inflections of grown-up voices) there seemed to exist (or to be supposed to exist) something like an attraction between the elder of the great-grandsons of the regicide general and one of the granddaughters of the wealthy producer of ink, an idyll surrounded by a discreet rumor and by a no less discreet disapproval (regretfully shared no doubt by the two principals concerned) and which, nolens volens (no doubt the disproportion be-

tween fortunes was excessive, if not scandalous), went no
further.

Besides that cat whose kittens she dispatched with an in-
tractable ferocity, and that brother with his livid, bald
skull, that maid with her narrow, ravaged face apparently
made of yellow clay stamped with that savage expression
(as if she had endured some unforgettable offence worse
than poverty, perhaps (who can ever tell, in these lost
villages?) something like a rape, as a child—or rather,
more likely, not a rape in the flesh but as if life itself once
and for all inflicted some irreparable wound upon her)
shared not strictly speaking her affection but her fate with
the strange creature which, more than the starveling and
always pregnant cat, seemed a transposition into the an-
imal kingdom of her own condition in the silent form of
a tortoise which appeared (or rather materialized) out of
its lair in the garden upon hearing (but only when uttered
by this one mistress) its name (for she had given it a
name—and not Zoé, or Toutoune, or Zezette, or some
other conventional name bestowed upon domestic animals, but a woman's name, a friend's name, Catherine if
I remember, she herself was named Thérèse), coming out
then, or rather shoveling its curving fin-shaped paws to
advance that carapace with its polygonal motifs out of
which stretched the wedge-shaped reptile head, like the

prow of some ship, protected by tiny gray scales, its eyes shielded by delicate silken lids and its notch-like mouth that silently snapped up and swallowed the lettuce leaves. As if between the creature surviving from prehistoric times and the woman bending over it her impenetrable countenance of desiccated leather with the same fierce tenderness as when she tended Maman there existed a sort of pact or occult link, a silent connivance, like some age-old alliance stronger than time, stronger than death.

Surrounded on all sides by the dull roar of the anarchic urban fabric, the hospital, with its identical pavilions except for two or three more recent ones of a brutal modernism, and its monastic, silent courtyards, constituted a sort of island in the midst of the tumultuous fragile chaos like a sort of self-contained scaled-down universe, enameled and shiny from its obstetric service to its morgue, offering as though in miniature (or in some sort of resumé) the human machine in all its successive states from birth to final agony, including every possible deviation and anomaly until its definitive corruption.

· · ·

Hideous wallpaper probably dating from the previous generation and which it had doubtless not been considered necessary to change in a bedroom temporarily occupied by a child but which, though at the time I was indifferent to its ugliness, must to some degree (if only by my habit of recognizing it again each summer?) have made a lasting impression and which I still seem to see in every detail as if, once the candle was blown out and in the suffocating heat of the September nights, I could vaguely feel rather than see around me the black splotches of those giant poppies on alternate sides of their pale hairy stems, spiraling up against a gray-green background: vague shapes which were inseparable in the darkness from the buzzing of some insect (although my aunt who accompanied me until I was in bed took precautions, before blowing out the candle, to ignite in a saucer one of those cones, I think they were called eucalyptus, their pungent smell in which the odor of new-mown hay mingled with that of incense persisting for a moment, struggling against the sickening scent of melted wax left by the extinguished candle) bumping against the mosquito netting surrounding my bed, while through the window came the night sounds of the countryside, the deafening racket of the crickets suddenly breaking off as though to give way to the barking of dogs answering each other from farm to farm, furious, outraged or plaintive as children's sobs (tenuous or remote sounds to which, later on, when the

Society Beach was replaced by the concrete cube known as the Casino, were added late at night the occasional squeal of brakes and tires on the curve at the bottom of the hill, the riders in the early trolleys the next morning contemplating, half-dismembered or overturned, the remains of what had been an automobile scattered among the vines bordering the road).

And, on windy days, as if someone were trying to force it open, the harsh scraping against the window grille of a branch at the end of the row of those rather sinister trees, half-cypress, half-cedar, which shaded the garden along the outer wall.

Inhaling the mingled odors of the pines and the fig trees, combined during the grape harvest with the thick, rather sticky smell of the fermenting must which permeated the motionless warm air of the moribund summer where, at twilight, the carts filled with the last tubs passed, the bare legs of the little girls who had been picking the grapes hanging over the side, gilded by the setting sun and speckled mauve by the grapes, swaying with the movement of the cart like a colorful laughing fringe.

．　．　．

Period when after the Second World War a certain cultural evolution of the members of the city council (or of their advisers) and of the café patrons led them to repudiate their earlier repudiation for the sake of a rehabilitation of what they now knew (or thought they knew) were the town's true artistic values (that is, the monuments or simply the houses which their predecessors had not yet had time to destroy: ramparts, palaces, old façades), sparing (doubtless because of the expense) the Corinthian courthouse and the bronze dignitary (surrounded now, in the fashion of spas everywhere, with banks of flowers and palms) but on the other hand merciless with regard to the spidery iron and glass rotunda with its graceful dragonfly marquee replaced by D. GOUGOL or his heirs (or some buyer), the whole structure, its transparencies, its wing-cases, its linen curtains and its Viennese orchestras supplanted by a yellow-painted cement structure roofed, according to the norms of the local style expected (or presumed to be expected) by the tourists (like the banks of flowers and palms) by smart pink tiles.

As if, in a second period and by an inverse reflex or a backwash effect, the town (or at least the advisers of the members of the city council, the café patrons and the contractors) had now no longer, as in the Belle Époque, counted on "imported" embellishments like the Corinthian capitals or a small-scale Crystal Palace, but had proudly resolved to affirm an architectural style likely to

satisfy both local pride and the tourist appetite for Mediterranean exoticism.

The private room to which I was finally assigned was
about ten feet square. Its walls were enameled not white
but gray with a touch of blue to shoulder height, and pale
beige up to the ceiling. To the left of the bed, light spilled
into the room through a big uncurtained window that
had an outdoor wooden blind which could be worked
from inside the room but the mechanism of which was
broken (or which I may have operated as clumsily as I
managed the device which allowed the upper third of the
bed to be raised or lowered, either at mealtimes or, when
my condition gradually improved, to read more com-
fortably, or on the occasion of a visit), my entire life as a
patient being concentrated on a host of these tiny details,
as for example the business of washing, for though each
room was provided with a sink, the fact that there was no
bidet made it difficult if not impossible to wash the middle
part of one's body, the sink being so high that it made
any efforts in respect to this area altogether acrobatic, so
that what the nurse called my *toilette* consisted of her
rubbing my chest and legs with a wet bath-glove, but
when I remarked to this nurse on the odd absence of this
indispensable accessory, she replied in a tone of sudden
indignation that every effort Monsieur had been made to

furnish the rooms properly but then the patients yes
Monsieur do you know what they did well they made *caca*
in the bidets, using (instead of "their excrement" or "their
needs" or some other ordinary expression) that crude
childish word by means of which doubtless, in her mind,
she was clearly telling me (as moreover an eminent surgeon later explained to me quite seriously) that for the
hospital personnel, from the "lowest" nurse to the "highest" administrator, a patient is regarded as a minor, if not
in fact as a child, with mental capacities diminished to the
point where he is no longer capable of making decisions
or even of grasping the meaning of words used by adults,
considerations which seemed to include as well, in my
nurse's mind, a condescension inspired by her profession
which she doubtless regarded as a social promotion permitting her to patronize those patients making "caca" in
the bidets.

In any case, finding myself treated in this fashion, my
toilette being limited to the most summary friction, em-
barrassed as I was to drag with me the sort of chromium-
plated steel scaffolding on which was hung the vessel the
contents of which filtered drop by drop into a vein of my
wrist, this vessel made of some sort of plastic at once
transparent and opaque, a grayish-white substance which
grew increasingly wrinkled, finally coming to resemble
those pig bladders that used to be in the pork butcher's
window. As for the system dispensing oxygen, it was possible, during my washing sessions, to unhook it from a

sort of plug set in the wall at the head of my bed and to plug it back in afterwards, an arrangement of pipes and tubes having been devised for this purpose in the pneumology pavilion. Yet it was quite painful to carry, the tube attached to the wall reaching from behind under my chin where it divided into two narrower branches that, passing behind my ears, came together again at the level of my nostrils into which they were crammed. As a matter of fact, after a few days, the skin between my ears and my skull became so irritated (for I had to keep this apparatus on, even when sleeping) that it was necessary to put a wad of cotton on each side of my head. Contrasting with the uniform grayish-white of the walls, of the furniture and of all the hospital equipment around me, this or rather these slender twin tubes were ultramarine blue.

Still, I imagine, because of that feverish state which gave me the sense of being under a sort of bell through which what was happening outside reached me in only the vaguest way, which is to say that it was impossible for me to establish coherent relations between cause and effect (between before or after), as for example in the course of those veritable expeditions constituted by my conveyance to the radiology service: the agreeable sensation of fresh air, chill—this was still only the first two weeks of March—on my face, coming out of the stuffy atmosphere of the room: wrapped in a blanket and sitting in the wheelchair pushed (impetuously, it seemed to me: a joyous impetuosity but perhaps I was attributing a joy and

a gayety to him which was merely the effect of that fresh
air, the pleasure of no longer finding myself shut up with
that coquettish and terrifying Punchinello? ...) ...
pushed by the big mulatto male nurse (probably from the
Caribbean) who came for me every two days: a veritable
journey (this service was located a long way from the
pneumology pavilion) through a succession of corridors
and elevators, their huge cabs capable of holding beds,
wheelchairs and hospital personnel proceeding from one
service to the next and whose chatter reached me in dis-
parate fragments, so that I wondered if I should connect
a certain phrase uttered between two floors by a woman's
voice, as for example: "How lovely she was with all those
flowers around her!", a phrase which could equally well
allude to a bride who was a friend of the nurses or to a
corpse on her bed in the morgue, with the encounter a
little previously (or a little subsequently) in the crosswalk
of a courtyard (visible to me only from the waist up, the
bottom half of their bodies concealed by a privet hedge)
of three young people, two girls and a young man (or the
opposite) between fifteen and twenty, walking in single
file in quick step (or at least it seemed quick to me, like
the spring air, the gait of my attendant, the outside world
altogether), each one carrying a big bunch of flowers, their
faces (in accord with that vaguely military stride) express-
ing neither sadness nor gayety, simply (the young man's
as much as those of the girls) inexpressive (they might
just as well have been going to some party) and vanishing

almost immediately from my sight—and nothing else, except on the way back, in the elevator, that woman's voice behind me, just as the big mulatto was pushing my wheelchair out of the elevator, speaking these words: ". . . so lovely with all those flowers around her!" which could logically, in such a place (a hospital) refer only to a corpse lying in the morgue among a profusion of roses and chrysanthemums: as for knowing whether a link existed between that corpse and the bouquets carried by the three young people at quick step, only the word "flower" could mean such a thing, but in my incapacity to remember if that apparition had occurred on my way to the X-ray service (which then might have made it possible that the same flowers were involved—the wait at the radiology service lasting sometimes more than an hour), I could not manage, through my glass bell, to locate things precisely in time, my mind retaining nothing but the pairing of the two words: flowers and death.

On reflection, I think that it was not only the rapid sight of the three young people carrying bouquets and (before? afterwards?) the few words overheard in the elevator which provoked in me that classical association of words, but even perhaps (or in addition), the same afternoon, in the corridor where the patients to be X-rayed were waiting their turn, lined up on one side, abandoned by their attendants, the strange apparition of what could not exactly be called a bed on wheels since the mattress was at virtually the same height as the heads of the two male nurses who were pushing a sort of impressive-looking machine consisting of steel tubes from which was somehow suspended, under a blanket pulled up to the neck and scarcely revealing the shape of a body whose head resting on a pillow was not, as might have been expected, the shrunken and half-cadaverous skull of a deathly ill patient but on the contrary (which made the scene even more disconcerting or more alarming) that of a woman of forty at most and not only in an apparent state of good health but actually pink and fresh-faced, surrounded by a mass of blond hair as impeccably waved as if she had just left the hairdresser, her face impassive, not smiling but somehow suffused with serenity (if not even perhaps with a certain contentment), as if aware of a kind of homage which was the translation of the inaudible thrill of dread her passing provoked on the faces of the waiting patients with their hitherto resigned, gloomy stares, as though suddenly alarmed, at once terrified and incredulous, as if, in their minds, the revelation of some dreadful disease necessitating such a scaffolding had suddenly displaced any other concern, any other pain, while they followed in silence the silent passage of the impressive-looking machine mounted on its silent rubber wheels and guided by the two silent male nurses wearing sandals, and of which the steel tubes, as though by a kind of theatrical refinement, were painted not that uniform gray prescribed for all hospital apparatus but a bright yellow, as if it was a matter of distinguishing the terrible machine in this way from the ordinary hospital equipment, as if a sort of ceremony were occurring here, the patient or rather the effigy still as motionless and almost smiling as those embalmed remains of some saint or of some blessed creature exhibited on the religious holidays, resting on the shoulders of some vigorous bearers and seeming to float over the crowd of the faithful on some sort of flower-strewn litter, made up, decorated, or repainted all over again each time.

(Simply busts sometimes in the center of a litter carried at arm's length, cut off at chest level, the shoulders covered in gold leaf and in the center, under the face with its fixed eyes, a sort of little oval window behind which, protected by a pane of glass, appear three or four grayish little bones set on a red velvet cushion. Sometimes only a shard of bone. Sometimes too something like a shaving or rather a splinter of wood (The Holy Cross?), but in that case no painted face: a sun with gold rays (monstrance?) surrounding the little window mounted on a base held between the hands of a priest in a white robe with a gold-embroidered white silk cape as well.)

· · ·

Remembering those cadavers wrapped (swathed) in linen, as though trussed up and laid out on litters, borne at night through the narrow dimly-lit streets of Benares and which (on the shoulders of muscular bearers) seemed somehow to float rather than to be carried on the tumultuous surface of the crowd stirred by sudden eddies (parents, friends, paid bearers or mourners—or simply the curious?); burial or rather the ceremony of burial: as a matter of fact I was told that the bodies were carried only this far down to the Ganges where they would remain on the bank, half immersed (taken away by boats at dawn, the next day in fact I saw three or four of them, grayish bundles lapped by the waves) until evening when they would then be burned: the escorting crowd not meditative in the Western manner but noisy, one or several dissonant chants rising from that confused or rather frenetic agitation which might just as well have suggested some festivity or other; a little later moreover, while we were watching from a terrace, there was one of those stakes on which we could still make out the mostly charred shape of a body which with the help of long rods two men were busily turning as if on a grill, and you could hear in the darkness, from another terrace gaily decorated with lanterns, other chants rising, harmonizing, accompanied by stringed instruments, and our guide explained that a wedding was being celebrated over there.

.   .   .

(Again: shrieking human clusters limbs legs arms waving around the edges seemed that August 15 to bristle from those *baladeuses* towed by the trolleys, their unbleached canvas curtains flapping like flags as if they themselves were participating in that noisy merriment you could hear approaching, swelling, exploding violently when the trolley and its trailer passed right through the villa-stop, then diminishing, fading out, letting the resinous scent of the pines close over the somnolent afternoon, the somnolent silence of the garden where the sea breeze sometimes made the delicate leaves of her mimosas tremble above the iris borders with their leaves shaped like yataghans and their pale mauve blossoms, thick clumps of rose-laurels, the chaise longue with the faded upholstery brought out just in case, empty beside the fountain, if its usual occupant was feeling too tired and had preferred to remain indoors, or to wait until the stifling heat had diminished toward evening.)

Just as he seemed to concentrate with hallucinatory effort what little physical strength and whatever intellectual faculties he had left in order not to waver, calculating with great care the distance to be covered between his bed and the door of the bathroom or the distance separating his hand from the glass he wanted to pick up, then the glass from his lips, he seemed to practice that same principle of economy in affective relations, behaving the same way with his visitors, evidently his children: each one in turn and doubtless taking time off from their work—or holiday: two men already middle-aged, apparently foremen or truck drivers, and a woman still young but with a worn face, all three in worn clothes (the woman wearing frayed slacks and low-heeled shoes), their low voices and respectful attitudes (he did not ask them to sit down—not even the woman) contrasting with the garish red velvet pajamas out of which emerged, authoritarian, imperial even, like the head of some old king, some margrave exhumed from a medieval legend, the fleshless head with its aquiline profile crowned with that silver crest he continually smoothed all day long with a maniacal or mad coquetry using a little tortoise-shell comb he would then put away in the breast pocket of his bathrobe, a scene which in my half-conscious state I managed to register only vaguely, wondering all the same if the whispering, no word of which was audible, failed to reach me because of that state of severe filial respect which still subsists in certain lower-class families or because of a certain timidity (or even dread) betrayed by the furtive glances one or the other of them shot toward the complicated set of tubes to which I was attached, the visitors finally leaving without kissing him (except the woman), murmuring some kind of timid greeting in my direction before hurrying (or rather fleeing) through the door, after which there was silence once more broken only by the comings and goings of the nurses carrying the thermometers and the medications for the night that was falling, the day simply a little grayer, the window, finally, altogether black.

I asked the nurse who brought me my lunch to do me a favor and open the little package of peanuts which was there on the tray like the kind offered with the drinks served on airplanes, the cellophane wrapping of which I have never managed to unseal, whereupon, picking it up and tearing it open right away (it was the same nurse— belonging to the ancillary service, who had informed me with vengeful scorn that when an effort had been made to install bidets, the patients had immediately made "caca" in them), she asked me with great condescension if I had never done any traveling—to which I replied unwilling to annoy her: Yes, certainly: a little . . .

(. . . Yes, certainly, a little: the emotion renewed each time when after long hours in the plane which seems motionless over the featureless ocean the traveler looking up from the book or the magazine he is leafing through suddenly realizes that up ahead the entire horizon is barred by a coast—or rather a continent—all of a sudden materializing out of nowhere, and occurring not under the usual aspect which a traveler discovers while watching the land approach but quite the contrary, for "it" seemed to advance slowly, or rather inexorably, in the secret and implacable way reptiles advance or lava flows from a volcano, like a sort of layer or rather a crust slowly floating on the surface of the globe. As if one had the privilege of watching millions of years earlier that slow drift of continents meeting—or separating from—each other, a crust not so much flat as apparently concave, clinging to the rotundity of the globe as though molded around it, as if, gilded by the sun and apparently deserted, a fragment of its rind was caught in its irrepressible motion, with its plains, its mountains, its rivers, its forests, all virgin of inhabitants, splendid, disturbing, suffused with that somehow cosmic majesty of matter subject only to its own laws, converging, separating or colliding with a fierce and majestic deliberation.)

Now, all I could see outside was the upper part of another hospital pavilion a short distance away and virtually perpendicular to mine, as ugly in the neutral afternoon light (this was one of the structures designed early in the century by the Public Welfare architects that can be seen, all on the same model, not only in Parisian hospitals but even in the provinces), with its walls of yellow industrial brick and its roof of reddish-brown industrial tiles—colors which nonetheless in the late afternoon, while the quality of the light was gradually changing, also changed, the roof turning slowly lilac, then mauve, then a plum color which harmonized unexpectedly with the wall which had also turned to a dark ochre by now. My fever had gone down a little. Still, though fastened to my bed by the same complicated system of tubes, thanks to the cotton wads placed behind my ears I was no longer suffering from that painful irritation caused by the oxygen tubes. After the evening meal (it was always the same nurse—or rather the same server) and the evening medications, I listened to the muffled echoes of activity in the corridor fading away, eventually ceasing almost completely. On the top floor, a balcony encircled the pavilion, its walls and roof now slowly shifting through a whole scale of colors, canceling out the dreary materials specified by the original architect, and, almost every evening, at this very moment, a man (an intern, a male nurse—or simply an employee?) dressed in white came out to lean on the balcony railing as though to enjoy the cool air of the twilight, remaining there a moment, his body bent over, not moving, perhaps watching something that was happening below, in that hospital courtyard, or simply resting there, going back inside, coming out almost at once with a chair he arranged on the balcony, sitting down, opening a newspaper but a moment later standing up again, folding the paper and leaving it on the seat of the chair, disappearing, reappearing a moment later with a sweater over his shoulders, sitting down again and returning to his newspaper until he put it down almost immediately to pull on his sweater, the same mute scene sometimes repeated by a woman who joined him, leaning on the railing beside him, both seeming to converse a moment (they were too far away for me to be able to make out their features), he or the woman sometimes making a gesture, until the cool evening air obliged the woman in her turn to go indoors for a sweater, the successive scenes which I eagerly followed (coming outside, attempts at settling down, first chill, talking) occurring in complete silence, appearing and disappearing like puppets until (the woman first, followed after a rather long interval by the man) the two tiny figures vanished inside, the second one closing the French door behind which, almost at once, a light went on, the geometric mass of the pavilion still distinct, silhouetted against the glass-colored sky until building and sky melted together, everything swallowed up in darkness in which a single yellow rectangle remained suspended.

An impenetrable and luxuriant vegetation of aloes and Barbary figs growing on the hillside below the terrace along the left wing protected the entrance, and through the tall stems of the aloes swaying their clusters of blossoms, the far horizon was bounded by a blue stripe on which, certain days, appeared and vanished tiny white specks which caused my aunt to decree without appeal that the sea was too high for anyone to swim today and we would not be going to the beach. The only amusement which then remained was to go down to the tennis court which the grown-ups left to us in the hottest part of the afternoon and where I persuaded my young cousin to join me in a set, ready to abandon her (calling her, quite contemptuously, "noodle"), which she accepted quite graciously—even with a certain relief and as a sort of deliverance when I happened to see young Espinosa gaily waving his racket as he headed down the bush-lined path leading to the court (the one who used to be called Gaguy but now Henri) who not seeing us on the beach had given up and taken his bicycle and despite the heat had covered the five kilometers separating the sea from the villa. I had recently been given a new racket and, unlike my young cousin who yielded with resignation to my sportive desires (already liberated, she was walking back to the house and, halfway up the slope, passed the boy she persisted—despite his evident irritation—in calling Gaguy), I considered with contempt the old pear-shaped wire rackets which, for the use of children or guests, hung on the hooks in the left-wing vestibule, a room always dimmed by the arbor of luxuriant rambler roses which protected it from the sun (it faced due south) and even darker (in contrast with the dazzling light outside, its persistence on the retina momentarily blinding the visitor) since, because of the humidity in this part of the house, its walls were not decorated by wallpaper, which would have soon faded, but by a heavy gray linen with big olive-green decorative motifs which darkened it even further, and where I always seemed to smell, mingling with the permanent odor of mildew, that indefinable odor of sweat and fatigue emanating from the bodies of five or six men who in the evenings at the end of each week sat there in a sort of ghostly silence, waiting for the pay which my aunt's husband counted out for them in that office opening onto the vestibule, the office too darkened by the foliage of a pomegranate tree spreading over its one window and where there stagnated, during the grape harvests, that special odor of the fermenting musts he was supervising, distilled in the classic Dujardin-Salleron, its two copper kettles gleaming in the shadows above his desk covered with papers: a mixture of odors—or fragrances—which, for me, were inseparable from that melancholy of late summer when I foresaw the moment when I would have to return for nine months to that Parisian boarding school and the at once monastic and military discipline contrasting so completely with the way of life which I had known till then and which gradually began to seem if not alien to me at least to retreat into a remote past (or a distant space) with which I slowly lost contact, so that many years later it was a kind of shock due not so much to the circumstances but to a gap in time and space that, from my saddle, I recognized Gaguy in the person of a Zouave wearing the legendary red chechia and in shirt-sleeves (it was April, but I can still see that cloudless sky, that clear spring sunlight which irradiated the scene) working in the middle of a group hastily digging some sort of entrenchment between Hirson and that Étang-de-la-Folie near the Belgian frontier where my squadron was riding to take up a position, within rifle shot, in fact, of that flowery hamlet (Eppe-Sauvage) through which we were to advance on the morning of May 10 to meet the enemy under the dismayed eyes of its inhabitants to whom we offered faces disguising our own anguish, our own fear we vainly attempted to overcome with a classic double piece of boasting: "Interesting to find out what it's like" and its corollary: "How will I hold up?", a curiosity which was to be fully satisfied when exactly ten days later and as though by one of those facetious ironies of History I crossed back through the same hamlet, on foot this time, exhausted, crestfallen, dying of hunger and thirst in the long and lamentable procession of prisoners heading for Germany, which is to say that as for the "how," it had been something like a wild goose chase, and as for "hold-ing up," it was possible to condition an otherwise normal young man in such a way that he would be capable of displaying not heroism, courage, patriotism or sense of duty but simply (by—but what?: degradation, idiotic van-ity, stubbornness, renunciation, or merely insurmountable fatigue of body and soul?) capable of advancing, riding a horse at a walk, into a death virtually as futile as it was certain—as for Gaguy then, already turning back on my saddle while we were moving inexorably away from each other, the last image I kept of him was that of his ever-diminishing figure leaning on a shovel, that red scarf on his head and waving one arm, the memory of that meeting with a procession of other childish memories coming back to me only much later (I had meanwhile sustained so many shocks and upsets . . .), when after my escape from captivity, taking refuge in the town where we had once both lived, I tried once or twice to find out, although not very hard (something in me was no longer functioning: I had seen too much, undergone too much: when I was heading home after an evening with friends, I would stare with a sort of alarmed incredulity at the audience coming out of movie-houses where merely by images they had been having "adventures"), hearing myself say: "You know, the one they used to call Gaguy," or "That's right, the Espinosas, whatever happened to them?" or even "No, that's not right! She was a devout Catholic she was always at Mass every Sunday Otherwise you don't think either Maman or your mother . . .", as if Madame Espinosa had never had anything but a kind of utility value: that of coming to make conversation with Maman or with my aunt in the shelter and, on days when the sea was too high, too covered with whitecaps, to send Gaguy to release my young cousin, excessively "noodle" as she was, and to take her place on the tennis court with me, a utility value not double but triple, for Gaguy had a brother four years older than himself, an interval separating me as well from the youngest of my cousins with whom, when the heat was a little less stifling and before the "grownups" (the older cousins and sometimes their guests—including the heiress of the fake Loire chateau) came to take possession of the court, he would come as a sort of advance guard to expel us, yielding sometimes to our pleas to start a doubles match generally interrupted after three or four games calling us ironically not "noodles" but "aces": They've been nice now be nice to them you aces Go back up to the house you can practice on the barn wall No it's not very wide I know all about it That'll teach you not to hit your balls all over the place you aces it's not enough to smash every shot Yes the barn wall on the right Great practice Go on now you aces It's our turn to play Right?

The tennis court my aunt's husband had had made by flattening out the hillside in the days (early in the century) when neither digging machines nor steam-shovels existed: a huge job of manual terracing the cost of which may have made it (the court) not quite deep enough back of the baselines—unless he (my aunt's husband) had abided by the dimensions in use those days when the game seemed closer to badminton than today's violent serves or smashes, as was suggested by that period photograph in which appeared (each furnished with a pear-shaped racket) several women in skirts that swept the dust and wearing extravagant flowered hats with equally extravagant bows but with blouses buttoning up to the chin, along with gentlemen who had taken the liberty of removing their collars and their neckties but whose shirts remained buttoned to the throat by one of those pearl buttons, the cuffs of their shirtsleeves also modestly buttoned, so that, with their white linen trousers bizarrely pegged below the knee, their silhouettes irresistibly suggested, rather than those of fencers, the vaudeville characters specializing in off-color jokes running around in their underwear on the stages of those Parisian theatres specializing in such performances, one of the sides of the court arranged by my aunt's husband as a sort of little grassed-in "salon" including a kiosk with four masonry pillars, a long-armed jointed pump, a cement bench and a few folding chairs backed up against one of those opulent clumps of long grass forming a sort of ample crinoline out of the center of which sprang the rigid stems of two or three of those cottony white "feather-dusters," a setting which, on the occasion of a photograph, had been used for the composition of one of those tableaux vivants people enjoyed so much in those days, the cast artistically distributed: a little girl pretending to work the pump handle, a boy holding a pail, three ladies sitting on the right near the "duster," among whom could be recognized Maman, that slight puffiness in her face which she had brought back from those idle years in the tropics and standing close to the net beside another of those vaudeville characters apparently accoutered in long underwear and sandals, the one who by his waxed moustache and his square beard I knew to be (or rather to have been) my father, he too smiling at the lens while tapping his leg with a negligently held racket, the photograph dated on the back (July 1914) in a handwriting with tall loops the ink of which, a wretched purple, had turned the down-strokes to a greenish gold (the yellowish paper itself foxed here and there with little fly-specks of pale brown)—the day of the month indistinct, whether it was a poorly shaped 3 or an 8, but what does that matter since in any case the figure smiling under his waxed moustache had only a few weeks to live: a sort of garden room kept just as it was years later (except perhaps that despite the dry-ness of the climate—but doubtless someone had watered it—a skimpy Swedish ivy was now clinging to one of the masonry pillars of the kiosk), as if the tears sliding down the surface of the photograph had caused only a little of that faint rust affecting the tennis-players in their fencers' (or vaudeville) outfits and the bright figures of the women in their huge hats—and now I no longer had to run at the start and at the end to catch the trolley when for some reason I was going to town, calmly waiting for it at the end of the Allée des Mûriers, but I no longer stood in the motorman's cab, merely passing through it to take a seat inside on one of the facing benches between which soon appeared the ticket-taker with as always in the crook of his elbow that same strange tray with two stacks of tiny tickets (one-way—round-trip), their pastel colors accented here and there by a brighter note (purple, indigo, ultramarine, cadmium) which he detached with a moistened thumb before handing it to you, the narrow track along which the trolley swayed bordered on one side by a thick hedge of those pale blue-gray, almost white bushes which no drought seemed to affect, like the ones which framed the path which ran down the dry hillside and above which I would see Gaguy's racket flashing back and forth.

As if nothing—or almost nothing—had changed . . .

"So lovely in the middle of all those flowers!" . . . no. Terrifying without a doubt, with her knifeblade nose, her papery gray skin which suffering had pasted to the bones of her face. But the coffin had been closed before my arrival. There remained the heavy intoxicating scent of the flowers and the stale odor of melted wax which dripped slowly down the candles.

. . . No one picked up the fallen olives, their crushed pulp blackening in the three brick steps up which, turning sharply to the right, you finished climbing the first ramp of the path bordered by those pale-blue bushes, and no one except the children paid any attention to the over-ripe figs with their wrinkled and almost black skin, the split flesh purple, grainy and terribly sweet, scattered a few yards farther on among the still-green clumps of grass faded to tan by summer, so that only the ants were left to dispute them in the powerful heavy perfume of the huge leaves. At the end of the Allée des Mûriers the trolley stopped at the foot of the big umbrella pine, its trunk tilted by the wind, almost lying flat at its base, covered not exactly with bark but with thick lozenge-shaped scales set one inside the other, colored a silky gray just tinged with pink in the center and bordered with a rough brown ridge. Between two of these oozed a perpetual glob of resin which first formed a big bubble almost the size of a gooseberry, sparkling gold in the sun and covered at the base with a sort of white powder before finally flowing in a long streak of gray tears, gradually turning whitish like bird droppings. In terra-cotta tubs, two dwarf aloes with yellow edged leaves crowned the doorjambs at the entry to the allée leading to the gardens where, in September, during the grape harvest, it seemed there perpetually floated between the rose-laurels in the motionless air the fine whitish dust raised by the car of some visitor—or simply (the drought was such) the hooves of the heavy Percherons and the iron-rimmed wheels of the grape carts. As if something more than summer was endlessly dying in the stifling immobility of the air in which there always seemed to be floating that hanging veil which no breath of wind stirred, slowly sinking, covering with a uniform shroud the leafy rose-laurels, the sun-scorched lawns, the faded irises and the basin of stagnant water under its impalpable layer of ashes, the impalpable and protecting mist of memory.